Scenes from endless summers

Robert John Goddard

Copyright © 2019 Robert John Goddard

All rights reserved.

ISBN: 9798623599452

ACKNOWLEDGEMENTS

Having an idea for a novel and turning it into a cover picture design is hard. I want to thank Andrea for creating a wonderful cover for *Scenes from endless summers*.

Andrea.price.concept

"We're taught to expect unconditional love from our parents, but I think it is more the gift our children give us. It's they who love us helplessly, no matter what or who we are."
Kathryn Harrison, <u>The Kiss</u>

1

Summer 1993 – Belmondo Hotel

Go or stay, girl. Do one or the other but don't hang around in limbo.

An inhalation of breath, a pull at the stomach, a straightening of the shoulders and a clenched-through-the-teeth urge of exhortation:

"Don't just stand there, Irene. Make your decision and act on it – now."

But a salivary urge was not enough to persuade Irene to move one centimetre so she clenched her fists and spat out:

"Steady, steady – go, go, go."

She leaned forward and shoved at the door. She tottered on the tips of her toes. She hovered on the threshold for a second before losing momentum, falling back on her heels and flinching as the doors, flapping on their hinges, gusted her face with draughts of sweat-and-beer-smelling air and not-quite-out-of-earshot melodies.

Oh, silly girl, Irene. Now what are you going to do?

Still frowning, she turned her attention to the music -

a blend of light classic and popular and she outlined a smile when a vocalist opened up with his version of "Nothing Else Matters," and she closed her eyes in order to get a sense of the dancers shuffling, so close, so out of sight but within the arc of her outstretched arm had the door been open, but instead of opening it again, she took a breath and swayed along with these invisible dancers, joined them in their slow, quick-quick, slow, quick-quick waltz and she set about separating thoughts from feelings and words from pictures and silently translated her worries into a conversation with herself.

Tonight, it will be different, Irene, you'll see. Just imagine what he will be wearing tonight. And what will he be? Will he be handsome? Will he be rich? What will he say to me? Well, whatever will be, will be, I suppose.

Another, and this time, deeper breath, perspiration prickling her brow, shoulders back, head up; then, the music stopped, doubts appeared again and, even if they stopped her in her tracks, they did nothing to halt the flow of her inner speech.

Oh, Irene dear. Mutton dressed as lamb you are, at forty-three.

She rested her open hand on the door and her forehead on its knuckles and tuned in to his face.

And, I mean, he's hardly Casanova, is he? You can find someone better, can't you? You can find someone a bit less scary. In fact, you should find someone who isn't scary at all and live a normal life.

The vocalist announced a foxtrot and the crooner sang:

"Every time I touch your hand…"

And then, without further ado, she found the decision made for her.

Irene pushed at the double doors and strode through them almost to the rhythm of a European tango and she prepared to face the music. Telling herself to keep her head down, her eyes to the front, and her face expressionless-to-bored, she remembered to sway "those hips."

"I know that when I dance with you...," sang the crooner.

The moment she entered this air-vibrating world, prickles of sweat formed and remained on her forehead, and her face flushed and she realised that this was a world she had almost forgotten, would probably have been lost to her had it not been for him, his vision and his daring, and their decision to act on it. The idea was a new departure, a trip into normality and back to the world of their youth, a time full of mystery, of limitlessness, of potential, of energy and opportunity and, most important of all, a world of discovery and rollicking in the excitement that accompanied it.

She shook her head, and her lips twitched their disappointment. The hotel ballroom was a bustle of shapes, shifting shadows and hidden faces, of menace and excitement, a dancefloor bathed in light and flanked with chairs pressed against the wall to give room to the dancers.

But he was nowhere to be seen.

Perhaps he has gone. Perhaps he knows what I feel. Perhaps…

Telling herself to stay calm, optimistic and cheerful, she placed herself in the darker shadow of a pillar and scanned the swaying and the swirling on the dance floor, looked for signs of him, his ease and grace, the curly, black hair and that dimple-when-he-smiled chin amongst the blinking sequins, the top spins, the twists and turns, the promenade steps, the patent leather and twinkling jewellery and she was still looking when the music stopped and there was a rush to the bar, an area that stretched away to the left from beneath her feet, an area of yellowish light, a jostle of people and seats providing sanctuary for danced-out feet and tired legs. To the right of this bar was the dining area and an unseen audience of shifting and restless shapes and glowing cigarette-ends and table lamps throwing shadows on pale cheek or forehead.

She recognised the symptoms of her own nervousness: the familiar film of sweat on her brow, her wide-open-and-staring-at-nothing-much eyes, a flush of the skin, and the furtive glances to see if anybody else noticed that she had been "stood-up," and the worst of it was that there was still no sign of him anywhere, and when the first bars of a new song signalled a dance-restart, there was an exodus from the bar and barely sipped gins and vodkas were abandoned and conversational gambits were left hanging in the air with the body odour.

"Did you ever have dance lessons?"
"What did you think of the…?"
"Will you let me lead the next one?"
"To improve technique, you could…"
"It's not quite my music."

And the few responses were stifled at birth by swallows, a collective thump of glass upon table top and the rush for the dance floor, and there was a renewed freshness in the dance patterns and moves so that the sound of rubbing and crackling material was enough to wake the dead - at least to her ears - while she skirted the dancers and the dancefloor and made towards the bar. Nobody had forced her to come and her failure to appreciate the changes wrought by time was for all to see – nobody was dressed as she was. The shop assistant had convinced her that it was fashion and that this summer was all about change – yes, even for a woman in her early forties, she had argued, it was a time for moving on and refusing to get stuck in the mud of grey and black, shoulder-padded business suits and plump instead for the bright and jaggedly patterned cotton dresses.

The clothes had seemed tame in the shop and when Irene spread them out on the bed at home, their simmering variety of colours was exciting and at first, she had liked the new and fiery red-and-orange look. It suited her hair and the way it flowed now that she had released it from its tied back style to a much more informal, freer, sexier, I-might-be-up-for-it style that brushed at her shoulders. But now she was here, in the lion's den, she was a fish out of water and her inner voice informed her, in no uncertain terms, that the words "beached whale" might be a more appropriate description of her and, if they were not adequate, "desperate and frightened middle-aged woman" might be a more suitable and accurate addition.

Regrets reared their heads and whispered their spite in her ear. It was all a bad idea. It would never work. Nobody could relive their youth. Once gone, it never came back. Mutton and lamb were eternally different and never the twain would, or could, meet.

Even the barman ignored her. He had his back to her and merely acknowledged her request for sparkling wine with a slight turn of the head before stuffing the shelves with bottles. She decided to ignore him, to show the world that she was above that sort of thing even if she had no desire to define what "that sort of thing" was and nor did she trouble to ask herself why this barman bothered her. After all, he hardly represented the world in all its variety.

She took a seat at a side-table for one, looked towards the darkness and scanned the shifting shapes in the dining area. It was hard to discern details but she almost convinced herself that he had to be there and unsuccessfully ignored the bitch inside who reminded her that he might have been joking and that she might be wasting her time.

That is what men do, dear. At least that is what he does. Will you never learn a lesson? How many times…? Yes, he is handsome and he is not poor and he has charm and persuasion and he can dance, but just recently, something else, something bad has got into the mix and I am not sure whether it came from him or me or did it come from both of us? Are we paying for our trespasses?

The waiter and the clink of glass and bottle, cut into her thoughts and, by the time the glass had been filled and half-drunk, there was still no trace of his long and elegant nose or his dark and flashing eyes searching for her, and there were no purposeful strides click-clacking across the floor, no masterful requests to dance that could not be refused. And yet, he had promised that he would come for her. But as soon as he said, "I promise," feelings of grief and disappointment surfaced and memories came to meet her and her heart sank. The words "I" and "promise" were associated with a variety of negative emotions and the end of lines and roads. Every "promise" she had ever heard from loved ones – father, mother and significant "others", stuck in her throat and made her want to be sick.

She decided to have one more glass of wine and she allowed her mind to drift away from her date and merely raised her arm and shouted her request to the dreadful barman's back. She loved Budleigh Salterton and was not going to allow it to become her almost beautiful, almost favourite or almost-anything-else resort because of a man. She would certainly not allow him to alter her memories of Budleigh from magical to almost magical or from perfect to almost perfect.

After all, her memories of Budleigh were those special childhood memories that most people had, and they lay like photographs on a page, perfectly black and white, and perfectly still and she had learned to find solace in these memories when times were bad and they included images of perfect children bent over bucket and spade and seaweed-clad castles in the sand, children wading and dodging the surf and jumping up and down in the waves that washed and eddied around their ankles, her father's hand sliding safe and warm into hers while wading out to watch the ships disappearing over the horizon and all of this to the accompaniment of the sun warming her shoulders.

Of all the mental pictures she had, she prized these perfect images of Budleigh Salterton and, in particular, those of Weston Beach and its associations with picnics by the sea. No matter that unreliable memory served up sandwiches without sand, jam with no wasps and sea water with no jelly fish but she did collect rocks, both red and white, and she offered them to her father and she was always disappointed when, at the end of the day, she found he had left them untouched, unexamined, unloved, abandoned and rejected on the beach along with her love. Nonetheless, she still felt something special when she heard the word "west." There was always something else, not something more exactly, but something to one side of the word, something like feelings for places and relationships, for warm tea and biscuits, cricket on the green and her father whispering "I will see you at the weekend" even if she waited all day and he clearly had found something more important to do and he had never turned up.

How almost perfect it all was, Irene, almost perfect, so terribly and heartbreakingly almost.

The slightest of touches on her arm - more a draft of air from his moving hand than a touch of his fingers - pulled her from her dream. She got to her feet, stepped to the back of the chair and placed her hands on the chairback and braced herself behind this barricade. She was only there for a second and her head was spinning and her skin was burning but she stumbled after him and a few moments later they were revolving round in a bath of light and, at once, she was so taken by the music that her whole body, from head to foot, was tingling with the rhythm and she forgot her concerns, forgot the horrible barman and she gazed at her almost perfect partner, who was moving with such grace that she hardly felt the ground beneath her feet. They swung towards the musicians, brushed the dais on which they were sitting and she caught the eye of the piano player. He was a man, perhaps a few years younger than her, dressed in a frock coat of many colours, just like the other band members but he gave her a smile as they danced past and raised his eyebrows and there was a look in his eye that suggested he had asked a question of her but she flicked her head away from his and away from the feeling, an uncomfortable and unwanted feeling, of complicity.

The music changed and they turned and turned round the room - he initiating with a twitch of the body, she spinning to the pressure of his hand - and momentum did the rest and, with flying feet, she forgot everything, who he really was, who she thought he was and she heard nothing but the enchanting music to which her feet danced almost of their own will and then: slow, slow, quick-quick, and they were on to the foxtrot.

"I've been dreaming of this moment," she said.

"How long have you been sleeping?"

"Forever," she said.

And her eyes stared up into his almost perfect eyes and lost themselves and she hoped upon hope that he would keep the wonder of her dream safe and she forced down the desire to look at the band, find the eyes of the piano player and hold them, look into them and fantasise. Instead, she looked into the eyes of her partner and whispered:

"Come away with me."

But she was not thinking of anywhere in particular. She had never noticed, until now, how his dark eyes sparkled – but only to the edge of his own orbs and then the sparkle stopped – dead – and his eyes scanned his surroundings, assessed the neighbours, the other dancers, the gait of strangers, the empty bottles and the smoking cigarettes and he judged them all and from a very dark and negative place.

The clock struck midnight and yet, Irene was not the least bit tired.

"I thought you would never come," she said.

"Did you think I would…?"

"Forget? I am not used to people keeping me waiting. My man never keeps me waiting. He knows better."

"I am not just any man," he said.

"What do you call yourself?"

"They call me Toni," he said. "Toni Burano."

"Italian?"

"British," he said. "Italian parents."

"You had better tell me all about yourself, Toni," she said, "how you come to be here on this velvety night, and sending my heart racing and dancing through this particular evening and in this particular hotel and wanting everything you have to give."

"Will you be here tomorrow and will you dance the same dance?"

"With you? We can always dance the same dances," she said, "but the music changes and tomorrow the music might be different. I don't want it to change. Not ever. I want this to go on forever and ever, amen."

"Tomorrow," he said, "tomorrow is another day."

"But you cannot fly…"

"Can't fly, actually…" he said.

"Until you let yourself…"

"No, no, it's not correct," he said. "The word is 'unless'."

"Will you still love me tomorrow?"

"Only if you learn your lines. You haven't done a good job of learning your lines."

"But will you love me tomorrow?"

Toni nodded towards the band.

"What about him?"

"Who?"

"The piano player."

"What about him? Do you want to shoot him?"

"Maybe I do. He's a bit full of himself, isn't he? He needs a slap."

"Now, Toni, you know I don't approve of violence."

"Don't tell me," Toni said. "Tell him. Tell the piano player. Nobody flirts with my Irene."

2

Summer 1993 – along the river

"Smooth and calm, isn't it?"
"On the surface, perhaps, but I see the occasional swirl of discontent, don't you?"

Irene frowned sideways at him.

"There are fish in the water," she said, jabbing a finger at the carp beneath the surface. "Can't you see them?"

"And they can be very aggressive to fish that are sick or…"

"Different in some way? Oh, listen to the expert."

"No need to be *snarky*, dearest," Toni said.

"I'm merely commenting on the depth of your knowledge, my love. I bow to your wisdom."

"What is it you want from me, dearest?"

"I want you to come clean, Toni. What have I done this time?"

The River Otter had burbled and flowed beside them since they left Budleigh Salterton for their walk along the river Otter to Otterton. Irene kept her ears open to his response and her eyes on that middle-distant point where she hoped upon hope to catch a first glimpse of the village, a place in which time never darkened the thatch of the cottages, where the wisteria grew over both eave and window, and the thwack of willow bat against leather ball ran with the stream beside the road and down to the river and the sea. She knew, but never delved into the fact, that the houses were largely restored-for-second-home cottages for wealthy Londoners but the thatched symbol of home, and her need for its permanence, had been a part of Irene since childhood and she was damned if she was going let anybody change it – whoever they were. This was her England, and she would make of it what she wanted and what she wanted was a version of home gleaned from poetry and a hundred village-and-horse-riding-squire novels and TV programmes with their dashing heroes and beautiful heroines, and this unchanging world made her feel safe and happy.

"Did you hear me, my dearest?"

"Yes, of course, my love."

They walked on in a heavy and pregnant silence, and they passed salt marshes, reed beds, meadow and pastureland. The nature reserve was their most favoured place in Budleigh and a place for their shared hobby of bird watching.

"Then you must have heard my question, Toni. I said…"

"You haven't done anything," he said.

"Then it must be the right time to ask."

"The right time to…?"

"Ask? Yes, ask about where we are going and things. Does all this have a future? You know, do we have a future?"

Toni smiled and nodded a nod that said of course he knew what she meant but when he opened his mouth to reply she stretched out her hand and laid it on his upper arm in order to bid him be silent. She tilted her head into the breeze and cocked her ear to indicate that he, too, should listen to this mournful cry of alarm. She pointed at a group of birds with long bills, straight and conical with a red base and a black top and, coming from it, was the alarm call, "Tyuuuu, tyuuuu, tyuuuu." There were about a hundred of them and they moved erratically and pecked at prey and ran together in one direction or swept through the water. Once the alarm was over, Toni said:

"And the right time for a little talk, I suppose, about where our relationship is…?"

"Going? Where our relationship is going? No, I don't mean that," Irene said. "Anyway, does our relationship have to go anywhere? Why can't it stay where it is? Didn't we decide not to have a future and keep happiness in the here and now? Oh, it's open."

"What's open? Our relationship?"

"No, the café, silly," she said. "Shall we have a cuppa? A bite to eat while we finish our review?"

The Mill, just off the riverside path, offered visitors, should they wish, the chance to experience the ancient art of milling and bread baking, to enjoy the food in the café and visit the art gallery. They sat at a table in the sunlight. They had decided long ago that if they were to keep their liaison a secret from the world, then they should merge with similar middle-aged couples, keep their conversation sparse, their eye-contact intermittent, their attitude of the taking-one-another-for-granted variety, and be indistinguishable from the long-term marrieds. The smiling, beaming middle-aged, those who held hands and stared into one another's eyes, were sure to be having an affair.

"So – the question is," she said, "whether or not it is working?"

"Is what working?"

"Toni - I mean us, of course. Are we still working or are we in decline? Do we still feel safe with each another? Do we still need each other like we did, you know, back then?"

Toni – the early days – those days when we knew that there was something more between us. We were not just friends, were we? You were bewitching and I was bewitched and together we plotted to keep it that way. And so here we are, a few years later, in a play of our own making, that we have produced and directed in order to save our souls and build an "us" we could be proud of. The summer has made us, given us warmth, the wind off the sea, swimming in the moonlight. I adore the summer flowers you still bring or still bring on those occasions when you still need to tell me you still love me.

"Still?" Toni said. "That sounds…"

"Ominous?"

"Yes, ominous. It's the word 'still' that bothers me. It somehow implies that we are running out of steam, running out of time."

Irene rolled her eyes and blew out an impatient sigh.

"We agreed to enjoy our relationship and have fun, didn't we?"

"Correct. And we agreed," Toni said, "that if and when the enjoyment went, it'd be gone forever."

"Forever and a day, actually," Irene said. "We did indeed say that."

"Is it over?" Toni asked. "Because I wanted to know…"

He leaned back in his chair, shook his head and opened his arms, and Irene knew these moments, knew that Toni was stimulated, allowing his thoughts to dance with his words, and along with those eloquent words there was that faraway twinkle in his eyes, so far away, in fact, that it could have belonged to the dark side of another planet or even another galaxy.

"What did you want to know, Toni?"
"Who was that man?"
"Man? Which man?"
"The man you smiled at last night."
"Me?"
"Yes, you. Who is he?"
"I don't know who you mean," Irene said. "That man over there?"

She made a movement of the head to indicate the dark-haired and young waiter. He had skipped out of the main building, surveyed the terrace and side-stepped to another table.

"No, not him. Are you saying that there are others?"
"Tony, my love, my protector and guardian angel, what are you getting at?"
"I don't know what to think," he said. "You are just…"
"What?"
"Just…"
"Just what?"
"Different."
"Different? How I am different?"
"You changed your clothes…"
"My clothes? I Changed them for you," she said.
"And you seem distracted all the time and you never talk about 'us' anymore."
"So - you think I am having an affair? Is this your problem?"

Tony shook his head.

"My problem is this," Toni said. "That he smiled at you, too. I assumed you knew each other."
"I only have eyes for you," she said.

Toni looked obliquely towards the ground.

"Well, that is nice to hear."
"Now you are being *snarky*, my love."
"Because you are provoking me, dearest," Toni said.

A hanging moment, the hanging of a wave before the crash, the calm before the storm, the silence of the music before the hammer blow finale and a moment of hesitation, a moment of fleeting fear.

"You are accusing me," she said, "of flirting with someone else."

"It was just a smile."

Irene pursed her lips.

"A smile?"

"With the piano player."

"I smiled with the piano player?"

"You both smiled. At the same time. As if you already knew each other."

Irene screwed up her mouth, chin and eyes and shook her head.

"What is the point, dearest?"

Toni thrust his dimpled chin upwards, tilted his head and surveyed the heavens while the twitch reappeared in his cheek. Irene blinked. Until that moment, she had referred to it as 'a' twitch or something non-specific, general and vague but 'the' twitch referred to a specific twitch, the twitch on Toni's cheek, the one he owned, belonged to him and which was now threatening and permanent.

"Forget it."

"Forget it? You accuse me of having an affair and then ask me to forget it?"

"A flirt, then?"

Irene looked down and wondered what she was dealing with, vivid imagination, false memory syndrome, the power of suggestion run amok, developing mental instability?

"Toni, you said you had this under control. You said you were back in the driving seat."

"*Prego*," said the waiter, slipping a writing pad from a back pocket.

Toni dictated their order, and the waiter jotted it down, his torso swivelling from the hip, and Irene tried to catch the man's eye but he, alert to every sound and movement and well-versed in these games of catch-me-if-you-can, was several steps ahead of her. After all, this was his territory, and the cafeteria terrace was his stage, and he was performing on it, bathing in the attention of his audience and enjoying his starring role. He pocketed the order pad and swept the used crockery from their table to his tray.

"*Grazie, signori*," he said and danced across the terrace.

Toni smiled and watched the waiter leave.

"Don't tell me I am imagining things," he said.

"I am asking myself what has got into you."

"I saw you smile at the piano man. You smiled at him, didn't you?"

"Maybe I did. So, what is wrong with a smile?"

"So, you admit you smiled at him?"

"I didn't say that."

"But he was smiling at you."

"Toni, dearest, where is all this coming from? Even if I did smile at somebody – so what is the big problem? People smile at other people all the time."

"Not in the way that you smiled at each other. Do you want to have an affair with this man?"

Irene stared at him as if she were seeing him for the first time. But it was not the first time she had seen him like this, not the first time she had seen his charm, his lies, his actions after thoughts fabulous, frantic and disturbed.

"Why are you doing this, Toni? Is it part of the act? You know, our act, our story? What are you doing, Toni?"

"Good question. What are you doing?" said a voice to one side of them. "I don't want to interfere, you know, but I make it my business to keep an eye on the town – keep it safe and keep it calm. Do you, by any chance, need a doctor?"

Irene could not speak for her man, but she was conscious of her appreciation of this intrusion. The conversation with Toni was heading for a bad ending.

"You can be sure of my absolute discretion," the man said.

When Irene raised her head, she found herself staring at the space between the discrete man's eyebrows and his hairline and, to her great surprise, she had already dubbed it "the thinking zone" and she imagined it forever open and sensing, collecting, analysing and differentiating.

"Please, feel free to come and see me if you think it might help."

The thinking zone effectively reduced the rest of the man to a supporting frame draped in a sailor's blazer and white trousers while both hands lay on the table and Irene noticed their crumpled-brown-paper skin and prominent veins, while the man's fingers were playing with the brim of a striped-band-wheat-straw skimmer hat.

"I am sure you will not regret your visit," he said.

Irene glanced at her hands and slipped them under the table when the man stood up and took several steps towards them and a gravelly crunch of his sailing shoes announced his arrival at their table.

"Forgive the intrusion," he said, "but people who stand out in the crowd will always grab my attention. And you two stand out. Let me tell you why this is, will you?"

He raised both arms to suggest a friendly embrace while his head turned from her to Toni.

"Name's Fletcher, Dr Fletcher – a medical doctor. Actually, I am the only doctor in Budleigh Salterton. I look after the health of its inhabitants. I guard the secrets of their souls. At the same time, I am the eyes and ears of the town, both its guardian and its protector. Very little can escape my notice. While sailing in the pleasant bay I can survey my kingdom."

"How very nice," Irene said. "I'm sure you look after the people very well."

The doctor pulled a chair from under the table and folded himself into it.

"The name is Burano if I am not mistaken?"

"Correct. How did you…?"

The doctor silenced the interruption by raising his hand in a way that, in Irene's eyes, had less to do with the military salute and more to do with the barely controlled movements of her childhood favourites Bill and Ben, flowerpot men.

"*Allora, lei deve parlare Italiano, Perche non ha parlato Italiano con quello li?*"

And he indicated the vague direction taken by the exiting waiter.

"Why would I speak Italian to him?" Toni queried. "When in England, do as the English do?"

"Question or answer?"

"Just a suggestion," said Toni. "Actually, my parents wanted me to learn English. They forbade Italian at home. Do you have connections in Italy?"

Dr Fletcher frowned into his glasses and disapproval drew at his chin while the dome of his head fell forward as if under its own weight.

"How short-sighted of them," Fletcher said. "You could have become bi-lingual."

"That was not high on their list of priorities. My grandparents had brought them here from Campania in 1924. They had always wanted to go to the US but their money ran out when they arrived in Liverpool and then the US passed…"

"Ah, yes, yes," Fletcher broke in, and he raised his arm in his Bill-and-Ben-flower-pot-men manner. "Those measures were designed to restrict the number of immigrants from Europe, if I am not mistaken…"

"Exactly," said Toni.

"And I am rarely mistaken…"

"There was never any question of returning to Italy," Toni said. "Learning Italian was never a priority when I was small."

Dr Fletcher shook his large head several times while the workings of the thinking zone revealed themselves in the ruffle of skin on his large forehead, in the tone of his voice and in the angle of his eyes – flaps fully down.

"And Italians are usually so sensitive to this sort of thing," he said in a manner that suggested he had not heard Toni's comment. "More international than we are, the Italians. But there you are, there you are… And I must say, you don't look like an Italian, but there we are."

"What do Italians look like?"

"And, of course, you're British."

"Indeed, we are. We come from…."

"Of course, of course you are British," Fletcher said. "Well, it is nice to meet you and if you have any problems while here, please feel free to take up my kind offer and come to my surgery. Now, I must be off. Patients to see this afternoon. I expect we will meet again before you go home?"

"I expect so," said Toni.

Fletcher smiled sweetly.

"Now do take care. I would not like our next meeting to occur in a hospital. Good day to you both."

He stood, touched at the corner of his skimmer hat and Irene and Toni watched him while he walked away, his head swivelling, chin lifting and arms swinging.

"Just look at him," Irene said. "And all that confidence and…"

"Ignorance and prejudice," said Toni, "does not allow for the opinions of the working class."

"Who does he think he is?" Irene asked.

"God, I expect," said Toni. "He'd better be careful."

"Why?"

"Even a God can become a cropper, my love. Yes, he'd better be careful or get an almighty slapping himself."

And Tony took her hand and they walked through the wicket gate and turned right up Maunder's Hill. They passed the water treatment works and followed the trail to join the coast path that connected them to Budleigh Salterton.

"And what was that about Italian parents and grandparents, Toni? Editing your memories or putting yourself in a good light?"

"A bit of both, Irene, my dear. Did you like my creation?"

She grabbed at his elbow and stroked at it.

"You're very imaginative," she said.

"Ah, the search for happiness – and if we find it, then how can we hold on to it? Perhaps, by creating our own history and telling it to friends, partners, work colleagues, interfering doctors and, most importantly, to ourselves. Memories of Budleigh – a story of endless summer. We can even believe it ourselves. This belief helps to give our lives meaning and it gives our lives purpose."

"That's a bit complicated, Mr Burano. Perhaps it is as simple as allowing ourselves to change and make something new of ourselves and tell it to the world. Now what on earth is wrong with that?"

Irene glanced at Toni and he was signalling agreement with nods of his head.

"Exactly. Absolutely nothing," she said, thinking of the piano player and firing off an expression of a doubt, and it flew from her stomach and out across the sea.

3

Summer 1993 – on the seafront

The mirror had been placed opposite the window to lighten and puff up their hotel room and, standing between the two, Irene was able to glance over her shoulder at the seafront promenade and preen and pose along with the parasols now tugging at their ties, flapping and waiting to unfurl their splendour and seduce the world. In the meantime, they clicked and nodded while knowing that their moment was arriving, their place in the sun assured by the day itself which seemed to be holding its breath in anticipation.

Irene slipped into her dungarees, dropped her purse into a side pocket, felt it knocking against her hip while tip-toeing towards the door. She pushed down on the door handle, pulled at the door and, glancing at the heap under the bed covers, she carefully avoided any slumbering-man-disturbing rub, scrape, click or squeak, sneaked over the threshold, closed the door behind her, resisted the temptation to open it again to check that Toni was still sleeping and crept her way through the still-warm and sweet-sleep-smelling corridors, down the stairs to the lobby and into the distant-kitchen sounds of plates washing and eggs frying. She clapped her hand over her purse to keep it steady while she passed through a side door and into the street and the whoosh of salty breeze on her face and a glorious oh-what-a-beautiful-morning sense of freedom and lightness of being. The English Channel was out of sight but she heard it lapping and foaming, clawing and roaring its way back through the pebbles to the water's edge.

As she skipped round the corner of the hotel, she loosened one strap of her dungarees, crossed the street and there, at last, spreading out in front of her, was the channel, its infinite promises filling her with the delights of being alone, the choice of this or that road and all of them salt-tangy, early morning virginal, untried and empty now apart from a milk float hovering, a paper boy delivering and a baker baking and, so far out to sea that its colour was invisible, a boat skimming across the waves. Perhaps it was Dr Fletcher watching and keeping an eye on his domain. She let her mind dwell, just for a very short while, on this man, everybody's intimate at the surgery but taking his pleasure by watching from a distance, and then she almost lost herself in the associated-with-her-childhood rush and crash of the sea, but on this day, the beauty of the waves brought up those intermittent but increasingly frequent feelings of guilt that here she was and she was doing nothing to make the world a better place in general and nothing to help the civilians of Sarajevo in particular. It was so unfair that here she was and there they were, so very far away from her own almost perfect life. Perhaps, she thought, she should enjoy the good life while it was good because happy times passed, like Toni had said, and in a moment of foreboding she saw her present continuous nudging forward between a future uncertain and a future imperfect.

A light headwind tugged at her hair and carried with it the welcome distraction of the pock-pock sound of racket against ball coming from the direction of the tennis courts, and the sound echoed through the morning light, and out over the sea. A man's voice encouraged and congratulated his opponent on a good shot, and from a not-too-distant radio, the sound of music drifted along the promenade, was buffeted in the light breeze and crossed the road to meet her. Strolling along the promenade, Irene was trying to decide whether the music was carried by the wind or whether it was carried by the light but wherever it came from, she thought she heard snatches of a warning from a popular song.

"God knows how you lied to me..." came the words.

"Good shot," cried the invisible tennis player.

"...and I thought you loved me so..."

Pock, pock sounded the ball.

"...but you are evil in a good disguise..."

A solitary gardener, tending to the borders on the seafront, looked sullenly at her as if she objected to an early presence disturbing her morning.

"Nice day," she said.

"Indeed, it is," Irene said, breathing in the smell of cut grass and wondering what time you would need to get up in order to start work so early. Certainly, by the time most holiday-makers made it out of their hotels, these gardeners, deliverers, early-risers and bakers were long gone and only to be replaced, once a week in winter and twice in the summer, by a shake of the house or hotel and a bang and a crash while the dustbin men emptied the bins of rubbish and ash – bang-bash.

There was a tap on her shoulder and a voice from behind.

"Is this yours?"

And will he be mine? Is this Prince Charming at last come to find me?

She took her time, wondering if the appearance of the speaker would correspond to the youthful tone suggested by the voice. His accent was southern, home counties, but the voice itself was crisp and suggestive of a person both bright and blustery. She raised her head and while she swung round, she kept her eyes looking straight ahead and she scanned the white buildings and the gardens and the streets sloping down towards the sea and the streams flowing beside them and disappearing under the road and reappearing as the slightest of disturbances in the sea and then – then he was there in front of her.

Oh, Prince Charming, you are too young and I am too old. For the moment, my future belongs with somebody else.

The bells pealed from a faraway church and the not-too-distant radio was still playing its warning and she imagined this apparition in front of her leaving her, walking away from her, down the road and into the sea.

But he looks familiar. Where have I seen this man before?

She suppressed the urge to touch at her hair and, anyway, she had not combed her hair that morning. She had simply hidden most of it under a head band. She saw that he was holding out his arms in the manner of a beggar but on his open palm lay her purse.

"You dropped this behind you," he said, "on the road."

A flashing of eyebrows, an opening of the face and a parting of the lips.

He is flirting, he's cheeky and he's familiar, early thirties, probably married, but where have I seen him before?

Irene kept her face unruffled while partly disapproving of friendly, younger men making eyes at an older woman and partly enjoying the idea that the years between them might mean the enjoyment of those little extras, additions and refinements that age could bring to a sexual encounter.

Oh, Irene, thinking of sex so quickly? Naughty girl.

She plucked the purse from his hand as if it were dirty or contaminated.

"Thank you so much," she said.

"We are both early risers," he said.

She slid the purse into the top pouch of her dungarees and looked him up and down for fear of looking into his eyes and allowing sex-related talk to ruffle her features or infect this early stage of their relationship.

"Do we know each other?"

"We met briefly," the man said. "At least, our eyes did. Remember?"

Irene shook her head but she was playing safe, had already, several times in her life, had the mortifying experience of waving at someone only to discover that the person was not who she thought. This man's nose, face shape and sensual mouth seemed familiar but without context, he could have been anybody. He was smiling, he was always smiling, could not imagine this face without a smile and yet his eyes were empty spaces, free of life scars and free of bitterness and there was a tragic innocence about him, something limiting – perhaps of his life.

"You will have to enlighten me," she said to the floor.

He smiled and, as he did so, his oh-so-cute-film-star smile gave her tingly goose bumps and his eyes sparkled and reached out to embrace her.

"Maybe your husband would not mind one dance, just one little dance this evening?"

"Toni?"

"Is that his name?"

He continued to stare, waiting for a reply but she was a long way from the seafront and remembering how nice it had been when she and Toni had been so young and discovering each other for the first time, he passing by late at night and yes, those flowers were so beautiful and how nice of him to remember and then the attempt at possession, the absence of light in his eyes, the ugliness and the apologies, romantic scenes, the vows of nevermore and, as time went by, the apparent recovery and they were still together after all these years.

"Yes, that's his name."

She stepped to one side as a group of roller-bladers shot between them and rumbled away and she used the sound level to construct a reply that made her look modern and just the type of woman who might be of interest to a bright and blustery one like this youngster beside her.

"You are free to ask him," she said, "but he can be quite unpredictable, can Toni."

"You've known each other a long time?"

"A very long time," she said. "In fact, we have known each other forever."

"Well, I hope Toni will not mind," he said touching his chest with his fingertips, "after all, I am only the piano player."

She noted his use of the name "Toni." It suggested familiarity or a lack of respect and she realised, to her surprise, that this both annoyed and excited her. Of course, they had met the evening before. He of the frock coat of many colours and the eyes that followed her.

"My name is Shaw," he said.

The piano-player looked deep into her eyes and she found herself returning his gaze and smiling in return but only because she felt comfortable in this world of theirs, comfortable on the seafront with the rising sun on her back and the sound of the rising tide in her ears.

"Nice to meet you, Mr Shaw," she said.

Soon afterwards, she was walking along the seafront and she became aware of a feeling that she had split her sides through laughter and, glancing at her reflection in a shop window, she saw and felt something positive in her eyes and she knew that when she and Mr Shaw met again, a delighted feeling would be there to greet her. There was a shout from behind and as she turned, he was already at her shoulders and brushing her elbow with his fingers.

"Call me Sonny," he said.

"I will," she said and she quickened her pace, fought off a shiver and drew a much-needed breath. He walked beside her and they walked in silence while she admired the sea, felt the wind on her face, his presence at her shoulder and, in no time at all, they were outside the hotel.

"And who are you?" Sonny said. "I would like to know the name of the person who makes me feel creative and inspired."

Is that what you call it?

"My name is Irene," she said and hurried across the street to the rhythm of her heart.

Back in her room, she stood at the window, looked down to the pavement and, while a warm sun rose high over the sea and heated her shoulders, she imagined herself telling her parents about her new acquaintance.

We talked of this and that in this light of a Budleigh morning. He has become my hideaway and he makes me feel that I am a first-time visitor in his life and the exhilaration of novelty is suspended in the air and makes me feel like a child at Christmas. Is this the chance I have been waiting for – the chance of a normal life?

Sadly, Irene knew that she had never spoken to her parents in this way but it was time to change for breakfast and something she had not felt for a long time appeared - those butterflies in her tummy woke up and started a dance all of their own.

4

Summer 1993 – in the ballroom

A straightening of the shoulders, a deep breath and another evening kicked off in Budleigh that summer and, for Irene, it was an evening like all the other evenings: dancing to his tune, appearing in the ballroom and playing the waiting game in the bar until he was ready to collect her and lead her to the dancefloor and into their world of side steps, of slow, slow, quick, quick, of smoothness and beauty followed by something more up-tempo with its hand wraps, spins, throw-outs and poses. This world of yesteryear, this world of wordless communication was both effortless and effective and it became their way of moving through life until Irene rebelled against dancing to the tunes of others, and her rebellion ushered in a period of dissonance. This began with a wiggle of her bottom and to everybody and nobody she announced:

"Must pay a visit."

"Is that practical?"

"I don't know. I did not buy this dress on the basis of how handy it would be to go to the loo."

"Hiking it up or taking it off? You can't skirt the issue now," Toni said.

"Very funny."

While Irene tottered and swayed towards the bathroom, she noticed that something inside her had shifted and this something was as fundamental as peeing and approached her as the question she had asked of him just a few days previously: was he still enjoying their relationship? Was she? Until now, she thought his possessive behaviour was quite touching and she didn't doubt that he loved her; but now, as if she had gone from dark to light, from hot to cold, her life and her identity felt so different, so off pitch and so grating.

Irene paused at the toilet door, grabbed the doorknob and held it – tight.

The past is holding us together but is there anything other than the past? What about dance?

Dance was a trip down memory lane, dance was how she recalled the fun and laughter of her youth, how she chose to remember and celebrate the heroes of the past, those, like her parents, jitterbugging the hours away until it was time to go back to the hospital or back to the skies over England to fight for a cause, and those, like Sam Cooke *twistin'* the night away and Little Eva *doin'* the locomotion.

Irene pushed at the door, entered the cubicle, stood over the toilet and faced the wall. She gathered up her skirts and straddled, crouched and emptied her bladder while the word "dance" brought on a memory of the will-he-kiss-me-or-won't-he-kiss-me moments of the 70s tennis-club disco and getting to know those butterflies that she named and could still name: the flutterer, the blocker and the contractor. Irene stood up and wiggled and pulled and she was out of the cubicle and washing her hands.

Well, if nothing else came of those dances, at least I have them as a pleasant memory and they taught me all about clothing and the practicalities of peeing.

And while she dried her hands, Irene reflected that the word "dance" still took her back to that time of pure and purifying thoughts, to the time when she was royalty, a never-changing and never-ageing princess waiting for the outstretched hand to lead her onto the floor where she expected and demanded the search for perfection in every dance and in all the myths, romance and fairy stories that accompanied them, that is: stories of handsome princes, of loving and caring mothers, wise and attentive-and-always-there-when-you-needed-them-pipe-smoking fathers, Kellogg's corn flake mornings when the sun always shone, the days never ended, everybody's teeth were beautiful and white and minutes passed unnoticed.

What a wonderful world that was, but suppose Toni loves me too much? Can I handle it? Is it me he needs or just anybody and anyone able to act as living proof that he is worthy of love?

Irene checked her look in the mirror, pushed at the toilet door and while she was weaving her way through the tables and chairs and the people going and coming she reflected that along with the myths and romance, the Kellogg's corn flake morning was an ideal to live by, a guiding light but a fragile construction – a house of cards that might collapse at any moment from the ever-present huffing and puffing wolfish threats that surrounded it and, while she was still without comfortable eyeshot, she noticed one such threat was lounging in her armchair. It was Sonny Shaw, the piano player, and he was conversing with her man.

Camouflaged amongst her fellow dancers and half-concealed by the movements of people and shadows, Irene wondered at the memory of the vibrant and flirtatious individual who had delighted her on the seafront the previous day and how this contrasted with the fixed smile, the listless posture and the dead eyes of the man in her chair, but once she was out of the forest of people and entering the personal space of both men, she was within the arc of their aura and their lamplight and Sonny looked straight at her and beamed in a way that suggested he was seeing the most beautiful thing imaginable. His transformation, reflected in the beam of love on his face, just took her breath away, and Irene could have folded up on the floor in response - but she didn't. Instead, she beamed a smile of her own, the one she had used since childhood to deal with bad or extraordinary times, the smile as a mechanism that protected her from the telling-off of a drink-crazed and competitive mother, or a raised hand and, perhaps, a punch from an angry and I-never-ever-wanted-a-daughter father.

There was a voice in her ear, a sound as distant as the moon.

"I'd like you to meet my wife."

"It's so nice to meet you," said Sonny.

She nodded and smiled and it was the sort of meek response that she had learned as a child, her way of dealing with the awkward and the difficult, with the raging and the shouting, with the red of face, the wild of eye and the crooked of mouth, but with her smile, her perfect white teeth and sparkling eyes, she could placate them all. The fact that she was now middle-aged, her teeth were less than perfect and her sparkling eyes had disappeared under a cloud, were thoughts as distant as the moon and hardly visible to her even on the clearest of nights when she looked up at the stars and asked, "How did I survive to be so sane?"

Mostly, she wore clothes of a juvenile nature and at that moment, so close to Sonny's eyes, she might just as well have been wearing no clothes at all, and it was all she could do to stop her hands from covering her most private parts.

"My pleasure," she said taking the chair next to him and sitting on it.

Then, something happened. The smile she had used since childhood, this old scab of so many wounds, simply disappeared, and neither did she see or feel it leave and nor did she consider looking for it because in place of this old scab-of-a-smile came something more alive, fluid, warm and healthy, and she realised that this new smile reflected his and their eyes were glued together. Sonny was shifting his position on the chair and biting his thumb. He put out his hand for her to take and then came the point of no return, of burning bridges and boats, of casting off and crossing the Rubicon.

"Sonny Shaw," he said.

Hardly two words to put her on her guard but her response sealed Sonny's fate and her destiny and, even though she saw the mistake like a roadblock in front of her, she crashed right into it. She knew his name and he knew she knew his name because they had already done the introductions on the promenade and yet they went through the charade to mislead Toni and give him the impression she and Sonny had never met before, and once this lie was told, there was no undoing of it. She could have slapped herself for being so stupid and Irene made flimsy excuses to herself for having lied. But the result was the same whatever excuse she made – she and Sonny were now a secret. Try as she might, that lie made them complicit and her independence, both of action and thought, was now compromised.

"Irene Castle," she replied, holding out her hand.

"Any relation to the famous dancer of the same name?"

His eyes sparkled and her tummy tingled with the pleasure of the hunt and there was power along with his smile, now a little smug smile, which told her that, together with their complicity, the smile would continue to widen until he had his way, until the hunted surrendered to the hunter. Irene blushed at the thought, and something shifted inside her when she saw, as clear as day, how insecure she was in the situation with Toni and, perhaps, something deep down in her had decided to test it, to break from it and live another way.

"And are you," she said, "the leader of the band?"

She was amazed at the cool and in-command tone of her voice, amazed that she was able to ignore his question and ask one of her own because she was actually flirting, and flirting's purpose came to her in a flash. As long as she was in control, Sonny was a toy to be played with and she treated it like a sport – perhaps a medieval one like bear-baiting - but a sport nonetheless.

"Nice of you to think so," he said. "I am flattered."

Flattered? By a once-upon-a-time spring chicken called Irene? She is not the most attractive woman in the world and nor does she have a good personality and wake up every day and organise herself for success and believe in herself and her vision because she doesn't have a vision and anyway her parents crushed that passionate and organised and successful person with their anger and their drink-fuelled tongue lashings before she reached her tenth year of life on this planet and she thinks she wants things to stay that way because it is simply too late to be someone else, isn't it?

"And where did you learn to dance like that?" he asked.

"Like what?"

"Like a professional," he said.

Irene stared at him while her fingers clamped the table top and supported her while unfamiliar feelings of self-esteem crowded round her and, for the first time in her adult life, middle-aged Irene saw the outlines of real possibilities for herself, the possibility of being the best she could be and it was dangling in front of her eyes and creating the illusion that she was brave enough to expand her horizons, to spread her wings and fly.

"Maybe you inherited your skills from your namesake?"

Irene jumped back into her skin. Sonny was pushing her and waiting for an answer. He had made reference to a husband-and-wife ballroom dance act from the beginning of the century. The couple, credited with popularising the foxtrot, reached the peak of their success in 1914.

"I'm not even a distant relation I am afraid," she said.

"Well, I am surprised," he said, glancing at Toni, who sat with ankles crossed and head down as though he was asleep or saying a prayer. "There is something of Irene Castle's rhythm in yours and I can see Vernon's energy, too. Certainly, I have rarely seen so much enthusiasm."

Irene felt her heart racing. She fumbled for words but it was Toni who raised his head and said rather breathlessly:

"It is very kind…of you to…suggest such a thing, Mr Shaw."

She glanced at Toni. His cheek was twitching wildly and whether it was "her" Toni or the "other" Toni uttering these clipped words between excessive pauses and with the rigid expression and the staring-ventriloquist's-dummy eyes, she could not say. What she could say, with absolute certainty and assurance, was that in the passing of one second, all her positive emotions of admiration for Toni, warmth for him and future happiness with him came into question in front of her eyes.

"We love to dance," she said in order to fill the fearful-anxious-angry silence, "don't we, Toni?"

"Yes, we do."

"So, have you been dancing together long?"

"Yes, we have," said Toni.

Irene smiled away her blues but was so unprepared for Sonny's next question that her response emerged as a myoclonic jerk of the diaphragm.

"Maybe you will dance with me one evening?"

"Foxtrot?"

"Tango, foxtrot, but slow fox is my favourite – it is all the same. What is important is that the dancers dance as one unit."

Toni was silent and white of skin, and he was covering one side of his face with his palm to hide the disfiguring and tell-tale twitch and Irene watched him looking at his shoes as if they had somehow let him down but she was unable to stop talking and the words were coming of their own accord in the manner of footsteps to a rhythm, automatic and thoughtless.

"Are you down for the season," she asked, "or are all musicians resident?" A huff and tut from nearby and Toni pushed his chair from the table, threw back his shoulders, mumbled some kind of explanation and swept away. She saw him in her peripheral vision while he weaved a way to the bar and she knew by the position of his head and the tension in the back that things could get nasty.

You need to act, Irene, before he has an episode.

After all, she had seen the child before, the Toni child, hurt, aggressive and lashing out. But even the thought of this could not tempt her to stop talking and moving to Sonny's music but while she talked, she watched Toni, at first standing at the bar and then taking a seat on a stool but wherever he was and whether he was standing or sitting, she saw and she understood that her absence left him unrestrained and she was going to be responsible for whatever happened next. Until that moment she had believed that life was random, that there was no rhyme to why things happened as they did, no reason to why some people got lucky and others did not – it was all luck and coincidence and these were not things you could or should take responsibility for.

What total nonsense. You had better get real, Irene, my girl. It is you who have the power to trigger events and you can do it with your presence, a look or a flick of your fingers.

And she knew that the ability to trigger things was probably connected to her own past, that the fuse had already been lit years previously and controlled her in a veil of fizzing and smoking forgetfulness. No, her meeting with Sonny was not random, a twist of fate that could easily be changed. Nonetheless, and here was the crux of the matter, random or not, her actions would have consequences.

Who is Toni to take advantage of you? You, my dear, must take control. Nobody should benefit from your goodness. You are the hours and he is just a second. His book is written but you can be the heroine of your own story. Change yourself and you really can change the world.

But force of habit prevented her from getting to her feet and stopping the inevitable. Sonny and Toni rose at the same time and both made a bee line for the toilets. There was a short distance between them but Irene calculated that their angle of attack would bring their torsos crashing together somewhere near the toilet door. Their movements were, apparently, random but every footfall had been timed to perfection. The few inches of noticeable space between Tony's legs was the same as the noticeable space between Sonny's legs and both took larger-than-usual strides and both men pointed their feet inwards and both had pocketed their hands so they walked with a rolling gait towards the collision zone and the collision, when it came, was the consequence of their story – Irene's story and Toni's story – and she had inserted someone else in their book and changed the plot.

And while the two men rolled towards the point of touch, of conflict, Irene speculated that although both were looking towards the floor, only Toni convinced her with his scowl and his palpable aura of menace. Toni was a veteran of the London railway network and he knew about the contact sport that was a stroll through the city, knew how to deal with the pavement-hog ploughing forward and unwilling to swerve for anybody. His was a cool, calm example of how to deal with pavement rage.

Irene allowed her mind to slip sideways and reflect on the way that Sonny might deal with a high-street showdown. She guessed he would prefer the sideways manoeuvre, the sorry-pardon-me-and-excuse-me behaviour of most city streets in England but Irene's chin dropped and her mouth opened when she realised that these two lounge lizards had other solutions in mind and these included a refusal to step aside, an I-am-more-of-a-man-than-you collision of shoulders. The actual contact resulted in a glaring-sneering-tight-lipped-and-white-faced Tony and a reeling-and-off-balance Sonny. Whether it was the force, the angle, or the look on Toni's face that bothered her she was unable to say but his facial expression shook up and dislodged her idea of him and Irene knew that the collision had marked the death of some things and the birth of other things. She would do her best to keep the good memories of him, the love that was needed, the love that protected them, kept them sane and alive and carried them both to health and beauty and safety, and she would never forget Toni with those gifts of his, standing outside her house in the dead of the morning, all uniformed up and she going along with the fiction that he really was a pilot or a policeman. She would put these memories in a safe place before they got discoloured and poisoned with exposure to the present. Yes, she would keep the good memories and the others could go to the darkness.

A presence spread over her and Irene looked up and into Toni's shadow. It darkened over her and, for the life of her, she was unable to imagine herself opening a conversation with him about how they could give up on unreasonable expectations and, at the same time, loosen their grip on a joint future they could never have.

"That is so true, man."

"What is so true, Toni?"

"No girl is perfect and no man is perfect, but the question is: 'Are we perfect for each other?'"

"*Good Will Hunting*?"

"Adapted."

Irene nodded and wondered how long she could keep the pretence, the memories and their love games in Budleigh before she loosened her own grip and watched their perfect future, going, going gone, woe oh woe oh woe...

5

June 6 1994 – in the gardens

I am trying to understand you, Toni, and paint your life in my head. I am living in your story as you are living in mine, and I am presenting myself in the most vivid and the most vibrant colours so that you can see me through the trees and the darkness and know me for what I am and never, ever forget me. Are you doing the same for me or are you dressed in grey or some other form of camouflage?

"What happened to Sonny," Irene asked. "How did he end up in such a state? Do you know what happened, Toni? Do you know anything about it at all?"

Toni was utterly engaged in this summer afternoon, one of bees, spilled tea and smears of jam, a café by the sea and all of this reviving and reflecting childhood memories of good and solid food, egg and cress, cheese and tomato, slow service and half-finished décor in high-walled gardens. A good many men, both white and crooked, leaned over the flowers and peered at the labels before clasping hands behind their backs and shuffling off to the next bed. These old men knew what it was like to shrivel up and die but this was their hour, this was their day, to remember those pals who had fallen in France in June 1944 and they made no fuss of those who could not be fussed over but the band on the bandstand urged them to meet again, to take a sentimental journey to the white cliffs and talk again with boogie-woogie bugle boy. He, after all, would not grow old as they had grown old.

"Sonny? Who's he? Where is he from with a name like that?"

"I've no idea where he comes from."

"Why is it important to you anyway?" Toni said.

"Am I not allowed to be curious? After all, he was there one minute and almost gone the next. He is lucky to be alive."

"Curiosity killed the cat, dearest, and who wants to take a trip down memory lane? You and I?"

Irene shook her head. Walking down "memory lane" was what these old folks were doing, piecing together what was vibrant in their past lives and clinging on to it. Irene shuddered at the quiver of every lip and hand when overcome by the events of the past, by the loss of youth, of friends. But what, Irene asked herself, did this mean for the future of these old people? It had probably been hard for them to free themselves from the past but, in doing so, had they also detached themselves from that pool of experiences which could be used to find a pathway through the present and into the future? But here they were. Somehow a reconciliation had been made and she saw that pride and joy had followed in quick succession and embroidered these old lives.

"You can't relive the past, my love," Irene said. "What's done is done."

"True, dearest. It's no use crying over spilt milk. Let bygones be bygones."

Is that really a good approach? Toni, let me ask you this. Will you turn around and look at your own background and will you learn to react to it in a positive way? Will you continue to let me work on who you are, and will you continue to work on me and who we should really be? Or is it time to say goodbye to our creation and allow 'us' to shrivel up and die?

"The past is best left alone?" Irene said.

"Perhaps it can be used as a yardstick of some kind? Then, we can see how far we have come, how much we have developed and changed since the beginning of our lives and our story."

She rarely delved into past lives of others and not because she had no interest but because she did not want questions to come the other way. They were awkward and often loaded with assumptions. "Where are you from?" was the obvious starter for ten. The question implied that the addressee was not from "here" and therefore a foreigner, an outsider and, perhaps, not to be trusted. But it could be worse than that. The motivation behind the question: "Where did you two meet each other?" was often used to sniff out or confirm assumptions regarding cultural or social identity – usually class. No, neither she nor Toni needed that meddling in their lives. It was their business and their business alone.

"A yardstick? Yes, you may be right," Irene said. "We can use the past as a guiding light. After all, the future is built upon the past, isn't it?"

And what of us, Toni? Have we freed ourselves from our "where-are-you-froms?" Of course, we haven't and it was stupid of us to try. We are not even the same people who made that original agreement except, perhaps, that we both have trauma in the past to escape from, don't we? Our backgrounds define us and we have to hide ourselves away in shame. Would it not be better and easier to be able to show others who we are, who we were and where we have been. Just look at these people today. How lucky for them that they have learned to wear their past with pride.

From the other side of the nearest high wall the music struck up and touched history with "We will meet again," and a woman's voice flew over the moss and the wall to reach them in the Fort Gardens. They were joined by several other visitors, some in straw hats, others in flowery hats and women in red dresses and men with their legs crossed on regulation cavalry twill, and the bees were buzzing and tea-cups were clinking on saucer and spoons, and seagulls were swooping while, just out of eye-shot, the sea was lapping and waiting and beckoning.

"So, what about you, Toni? What has happened that has made you what you are today?"

"Give me a minute," he said.

So, Toni, will you turn around now and shine a light on that place you have come from? Will you recognise me as an integral part of your story? Will I allow you to remain part of mine?

And yet, she knew him inside out and he knew her in the same way. But, for them, this understanding had not come in a rush of confession or a nostalgic look into the past, not all at once in one smooth movement. This understanding had come like the fox trot - slow, slow, quick-quick - and the pieces had come together to form a sketch with shaded bits and every time he told his story it changed its shading, its outlines and perspectives and this one was no exception.

"What is your earliest memory," she asked.

Toni began with a fidget.

"Those slats," he said pointing to the window shutters of the Fort Tearooms. "Those slats – they stir a vague memory of times past, times at Goyt Bridge; a boy

45

whose feet barely touch the ground, sitting and waiting for "Children's Hour" while his mother sits opposite, her eyelids flickering, the bottle rolling on the floor, a cigarette burning between her fingers."

He sat and stared at the flowerbed through eyelids that fluttered, opened and closed in an attempt to focus on some screen in his memory.

"He is weighing up the risks of disturbing her by removing the cigarette or leaving it to burn her fingers. On impulse, he solves his dilemma by ignoring it. He makes the decision to play in the garden, and he switches off the radio, intending to come back later and listen with mother."

That is almost forty years ago, Toni. How come you suddenly remember it now, that moment when you managed to stop the world until you were ready to face it – and on your terms.

"Sounds easy, doesn't it?" Toni said. "Just turn your back on what you don't like and never look back. But it was never as simple as that because the world never lets us turn our backs on it, does it? "It" meant any level of violence from a slap in the face from my mother or a beating from my father simply because I was there to receive it. I dealt with it by ignoring them or by living in a fantasy world of dressing up, playing the part and becoming someone, always becoming someone else. You know, don't you, my love, that I am the 'becoming man,' always changing his past, his present and his future and always about to be somebody else."

And very becoming you became, indeed. And you chose to take on other roles, didn't you? By dressing up, by playing a becoming part you allowed yourself to exist after the thrashing, the burning, the humiliation, didn't you? But what have you done with your real self, Toni? Where did you park it? Who are you now?

"And then, by the time I was 13, I realised I could identify with the characters of favourite books and I discovered the public library. As well as finding escape and solace in other identities, I learned to find peace in the public library by escaping into books. One particularly hot summer, I lived through persistent beatings from both mum and dad."

Oh, Toni, the words "mum and dad" are usually loaded with affection and love. How can you use them when this association is so misplaced?

"I found refuge in an elaborate story about refugees. It was so successful that I thought I was one. And then, I withdrew into a fantasy world and lived the life of a spy. I waited every day at the train station for the arrival of the London train. I would scan the descending passengers and choose one because he looked different or suspicious and I followed him or her home and I watched him or her carefully through the hedge. Later, when I was able to lose myself in books, I created a more permanent identity, that of Bond's friend and associate, 006, and always my escapades were on my terms and mostly had a happy ending."

"But you still liked to dress up in uniforms, didn't you, Toni."

"In the present tense, 'still like to,' you mean, and I am that officer, that pilot, that soldier for a short period of time."

"So, what had happened last year, Toni. What did you do to Sonny?"

"Me? What did I do to him? Nothing at all. We had a little 'tiff' on the dance floor and nothing more. Why would I want to hurt him?"

She allowed her eyes to skim over the newspaper cutting she was holding.

"Did you never read this article from last year, Toni?"

"Article?"

"Yes, the article about the attack. Did you read it?"

"I don't have my glasses with me."

"You don't wear glasses. You have the eyesight of a child."

"You flatter me. Mirror, mirror on the wall, who has the best eyesight of all?"

"Please…"

"Can you read it to me? I ain't heard nothing yet."

"Just stop… Listen."

Irene tilted the newspaper towards her eyes. The paper was soiled and tatty from the sweaty fingers that did not want to believe, the pressure of the finger tips that accompanied the tears, the fear of retribution, of being the accomplice.

"Police are trying to trace witnesses," Irene read, "after a man was found beaten and seriously injured on the Budleigh seafront last Sunday morning, authorities say. The 35-year-old was discovered with head injuries in the rose gardens at around 1:40 a.m. He was carried out of the gardens and transported to Southwestern Memorial Hospital where he remains in a serious condition, the Devon Police said. A passer-by had noticed the severely beaten man and called the police. 'His whole face was bloody; blood was coming out of his mouth, out of his nose, and there was blood on his shirt, blood all on his clothes,' the man said. 'It looked like he had been in a serious, serious altercation.'"

She looked up, searching for a reaction, a sign of regret, of indifference, but there was nothing, not a look nor a twitch but only a wide yawn and a hasty covering of his mouth and eyes that said "sorry."

"Det Sgt Yvonne Richards from Exeter CID, said: 'Detectives want to speak to the occupants of two cars which were seen driving towards Otterton just before emergency services arrived. At this time, we are appealing for anyone in Top Street or the surrounding area between midnight and 2.00 who saw anything suspicious, to please contact police immediately. Police are particularly interested in speaking to the occupants of a dark-coloured car and a smaller light-coloured car seen driving near the gardens just prior to the arrival of the emergency services. If you were one of these individuals, please get in touch.'"

Irene let the paper fall back onto her knees. Toni looked up and opened his arms fan-like in front of him.

"It's not personal, Sonny. It's strictly business."

"Toni, please…"

"That was from *The Godfather*. Remember?"

"Tony. Stop it. We are not playing games now. What do you know about this?"

Tony shook his head.

"It's all news to me," he said.

6

Summer 1995 – Saturday morning

"He comes to see me on a regular basis," the doctor said. "It's always about those headaches, you know, and he has memory problems, too. Difficult to put one's finger on it, give it a name, even for a doctor like me, but Sonny is not the person he was before the attack."

Doctor Fletcher raised his arms as though he would take applause but his generous gesture was wasted on Irene. She merely noted that his arms were behaving in their slightly-out-of-control-Bill-and-Ben way and was hardly attentive when he continued with:

"In fact, he is almost a different person."

Fletcher raised his eyebrows and while they almost disappeared into the vast dome of his forehead, Irene glanced into his eyes and noted the shadow of condemnation lurking there and laying the inexcusable fault of not-being-the-same-person-he-was foursquare at Sonny's door. She wrinkled her nose and nodded but she was unsure whether these facial movements of hers expressed pain or displeasure, agreement or disagreement; and anyway, she was already distracted by the street pianist and she frowned into the tumble of a familiar finale, its echo drifting over her head and making off in the direction of the estuary, and her thoughts drifted with it, to the seafront, the market square, the church or anywhere else where Sonny decided to set up stage and play to the passers-by before wheeling the piano away and, according to Fletcher, it was only on the bad days, the days of a throbbing head, double vision and depression that he did not appear in order to entertain both locals and visitors.

"And he was never able to help much with the identification of his attacker. Came from behind by all accounts. It is all very disturbing that such a thing should happen here - and on my watch, too."

Irene turned her face away from his and pretended to admire the flatlands by the estuary. She could not see the river but its position was boundaried by the cedars she knew so well, had known since childhood, knew they also marked the rising cliffs on the other bank and its Roman villa, uncovered years before. And while her mind flowed with the river, her thoughts – clear as crystal – floated by the fields and the flowers and the cliffs and they asked her why it was that she punished herself by putting herself in the presence of this arrogantly hateful man and she knew as she flowed towards the sea that she could no more escape from him than she could from her conscience, that he was her conscience and the person who connected her to the normal world and the person in whom she could confide.

"On your watch?"

"Yes, my watch. There have always been doctors here in Budleigh but this act of unprecedented violence happened at a time for which I was responsible, and on that night two years ago, I let a man down."

Irene looked into his eyes, saw the genuine remorse that inhabited them, and nodded once, twice, three times while a larger number of thoughts struggled to surface and, as they turned - a waterfall of conflicting and churning ideas - there was a rush of stillness and she pictured Sonny outside the church with a ring of people in support. For some reason she was unable to fathom, she no longer thought of Sonny as a *pianist*. He had been demoted by her to the position of *piano player* but, whatever he now was, he was currently enjoying that magical moment at the start of every piece or phrase, imagining the music he had decided to play rushing towards him and he lifted his hand and grabbed it, breathed it into being, gave it something that had been taken from him and that something was energy and it was life for him, so that from the moment the first notes emerged and flew over the rooftops, they inspired stillness, silence, passion and they moved hearts and minds and set fingers drumming and feet tapping.

"But you know," the doctor said, "I was there on the scene that night."

Is he looking for applause? Or is he looking down at his feet to remind himself of their existence?

"You must understand," he said without looking up, "Those policemen might be interested in speaking to the occupants of both the dark-coloured car and the smaller light-coloured car, but I know they are barking up the wrong tree."

Fletcher looked up, and with a light smile, he waited for the questions to come, the questions that must be in her head, questions that demanded immediate answers, the questions about what he knew, how he knew it and what he was going to do with it. But Irene stayed silent, smiled and raised her eyebrows in expectation of more, more information, more interpretations, more revelations and more supposition.

"Alright, Mrs Castle, I know that the car people had nothing whatever to do with this crime," and he leaned forward and used his large head to beat out the words: "The Police just have not got their act together."

"And you have?"

"My dear Mrs Castle," he said brushing away her barely concealed doubt with a casual flick of his hand, "a person in my position must always be aware of what is going on around him. He must also have his finger on the button, keep that powder dry, you know, and limber up and be prepared – always be prepared."

Irene watched him wondering whether he was an arrogant fool or whether he had somehow mastered the ability to look, listen and see what was underneath: the roots beneath the tree, the emotion that drove the composer, the author, the poet, and the abuse that drove the man or woman and every blow that hit or missed, that left its scars to seep and to fester, and she wondered whether these people, perhaps all people, Fletcher and Toni included, were simply victims of their histories - be that for good or bad.

"How do you know those drivers had nothing to do with it?"

The doctor studied his feet again.

"I'm as sure as I can be, given the lack of further evidence."

"Tell me more."

"And you tell me," he said, "whether you have ever been so troubled or so sleepless at night that a walk was the only option."

He looked up, smiled into her dumb silence and said:

"Well, sometimes I have. It is, perhaps, a doctor's lot, troubled as we are by whether or not we have made the right diagnosis, prescribed the right pills, overlooked the obvious."

The doctor clasped his hands together, let them thump to the table top while his wandering eyes suggested to her that he was about to make a confession.

"Have you never wondered what it might feel like to be the last human on planet earth, a sort of only survivor of nuclear war but left, not with ruins, but with the intact trappings of civilisation?"

His eyes smiled into Irene's eyes and they laughed at her silence.

"Believe me," he said in a way that suggested he really believed himself to be believable. "If you have ever thought about being the last man or woman, as it were, you should try a little night walk in a smallish seaside town like this one. You know, every sense you have is heightened. You find yourself wishing for any sound of life – and when you hear something you jump out of your skin whether you want to or not."

The church of St Thomas sounded the hours. Irene found them not in the least bit friendly nor unfriendly but she did find herself asking what sort of sound it was that travelled through the streets at night. Was it a wail, a hum, a rustle or simply the sound of your breathing or the wind or a faraway train whistling through the night?

"Well, on that night 2 years ago, I was strolling through the streets and on my way to I-am-not-sure-where when I saw a shape and heard noises in the rose garden. When I got closer, I realised the noises were the grunts of what I thought was a drunk or an addict thumping the grass with his fist."

When Sonny tinkled out the opening bars of "The Entertainer," Fletcher paused, looked up and into the middle distance for a second while Irene suppressed a real desire to stand up and slap the doctor's face and knock all his arrogance out of him.

"I am not easily shocked, you know. Doctors are not easily shocked at all, but I was, indeed, taken aback when I saw the shape was, in fact, two people. One was lying on the other and beating him so hard that the idiom 'flogging a dead horse' came to my mind and the flogger must have heard me because he – at least I assumed it was a 'he' - scrambled up and ran as I approached. The other man was twitching and shivering and these spasms indicated to me that he was not far from dead. I was myself shaking at that moment, and I wasn't even sure what I should be feeling but I suppose I was a variety of emotions at the same time and not one of them was positive."

The doctor said nothing more and his pause drifted into an embarrassing silence that might have been too embarrassing had it not been for the sound of Sonny's piano-playing drifting between them but Fletcher seemed to have run ahead of the music and found refuge or lost himself for a moment in memory but he rebounded to reality with:

"There was a chattering noise, and I recall wondering whether the noise was caused by his teeth – false teeth by the sound of them – but as I made towards him, I saw him staring at me and I have no idea who he saw or whether he thought it was another assailant come to beat him."

Irene leaned forward and reached out to touch his arm, to pull him back from this night walk but Fletcher stopped the slide and said:

"Yes, blood was dripping from his ears, nose and

slopping from his mouth. I can tell you Mrs Castle, I have been a doctor for many years and I have seen some terrible wounds, but these have almost always been in a sanitised hospital and never in the wild, as it were, on the grass, alone at night in a rose garden, but the professional doctor in me took over and I rushed forward, laid my hand on the man's shoulders and pulled him sideways into the survival position, but seeing that his injuries were so serious, I took out my mobile phone and rang the police and ambulance."

"Did the beaten man say anything to you?"

"He mumbled something before disappearing into a world – a kind of night walk of his own - from which he has never really returned."

"What did he mumble?"

"Nothing much at first. His sounds were voiceless, a sound of a baby's babbling that brought spittle to his lips but nothing of meaning until with an effort he said the word, 'p-p-pilot.'"

"Pilot? Are you sure? Is it not possible that…?"

"I was mistaken? It is always possible, Mrs Castle. Even doctors can make mistakes but that was highly improbable on this occasion."

"What was so special about this occasion, Dr Fletcher?"

"Oh, the night stillness, the silence was quite intense. Even the sea was silent that night."

"So – he said the word 'pilot' you say?"

"Yes, exactly. Pilot."

"Was anyone else there? Any other…?"

"Witnesses?"

"Yes, witnesses."

"Of course, there were no witnesses. To all intents and purposes, I could be making up the whole thing - even a man of standing like me. And our "pilot" seems to have flown. After all, that is what pilots do, isn't it?

But we know better, don't we?"

With a finger flourish, Sonny approached the end of "The Entertainer" and Irene imagined a shrugging movement of the shoulders and the piece came to an end and the echoing finale was drowned in cheers and clapping followed by a loud chatter and the chink of coins thrown into Sonny's hat.

"Of course," the doctor said, "Sonny has never given any indication of who attacked him that night but let me tell you what I think, shall I? When I survey my kingdom, it is important to me that I know every secret, every crime and every potential crime."

She was tempted to challenge him, to ask him why this knowledge was important to him but Irene thought she knew the answer. Because it gave him power and control. Perhaps, like Toni, the doctor had been bullied all his life or maybe he had been manipulated and hurt by others and now sought power in his role as a doctor to protect himself.

"It's important because I am a man of standing, a doctor, a pillar of the community and, as such, I considered it my duty to make enquiries," the doctor said.

"Why didn't you leave it all to the Police?"

"Because the Police have better things to do than investigate an assault. And let's face it, as bad as the beating was, it was just assault."

"So – what did you discover?"

"As far as it is possible to tell, there were no regular airline pilots staying in any of our hotels at that time. Of course, it is possible that a pilot was staying with relatives but why would he be wearing his uniform at that time of night. It does not make sense, does it? Or does it?"

"Why ask me?" Irene said.

"Because I also made enquiries about you and Toni

and what I discovered was troubling."

"Troubling? My life – troubling? Never have I used this word to describe my life."

The doctor raised a finger and wagged it between his eyebrows.

"My dear, Mrs Castle, whatever happens to you is the norm. However troubling it may be to others, to you it is just life, just what happens to everybody, except it doesn't happen to everybody, does it? Have you understood me?"

"I have lost you completely."

The doctor smiled his you-can-trust-me-I-am-a-doctor smile.

"In the same way that I have lost you, no doubt, Mrs Castle."

"But I am here in front of you, Dr Fletcher."

"Indeed, you are." Fletcher said, and he lifted his arms in front of him in that slightly-out-of-control-Bill-and-Ben way of his and studied Irene's face before saying, "I thought someone like you might say something like that, but what has happened to you both is very interesting. It is interesting because most people leave a vapour trail behind them, and this trail tells us a lot about who you are, what background you were born into and where you are heading next. The library can be a great help. They have directories you know and most of us are traceable. But you two, Irene Castle and Toni Burano, you are both an enigma, and doctors do not appreciate enigmas. I drew a complete blank and now I am forced to speculate."

"About what?"

"You are not what you seem to be. I found no record of you anywhere. I even used my medical contacts throughout the entire country but the only Irene Castle I found is our dancer from the beginning of the century."

He lowered his arms, inclined his head and appeared

to contemplate Irene's face for a while.

"Who exactly are you two? And why do you come here every year under what I suppose are assumed names? What exactly are you up to? You can tell me, you know. Your secret will be safe with me. But I can tell you this. You have a choice, don't forget. It is rarely necessary to accept life as it is. You can move away. You can change. Promise me that you will change. Please, promise me."

And Irene shook her head. Change was not something she desired, wanted or yearned for.

"Promises are words I rarely utter," she said. "Promises are words that often lead to broken promises, slammed doors and to grief."

"Then what do you want, Mrs Castle?"

But she was thinking of her childhood, of almost perfect summer holidays, of her almost perfect parents and she said:

"I fancy a nice cuppa, Dr Fletcher. Would you like one?"

7

Summer 1995 - Sunday morning

"How's life today, big boy?"
Toni nodded.
"Life's good, girl," he replied.
"I'm really pleased to see you again after all these years."
"The pleasure is mine. I have been waiting and thinking about inventing some kind of story to explain why I am dressed like this today."

His head accompanied the word "this" to indicate the clothes he was wearing, a white shirt with the rank insignia of a royal navy officer. A cap, dangling on his chair, attracted admiring glances from fellow breakfasters in the hotel restaurant.

"That uniform makes you different from everybody else, except that you are not really different from anybody else. But you are handsome."

"I am not any different from you. But I am a man and, like most men, I am full of hormones, and these make me feel invincible and give me the belief that I can achieve great things, just like you."

"But not unless we seize the day, captain, seize the day…"

Toni screwed up one side of his face and said:

"You are losing your touch."

"Really?"

"Yes, really. You haven't learned your lines and without your lines you cannot play your role."

"What are the right lines, Toni?"

It was *'carpe diem'* they actually said, wasn't it?"

"Are we in the same film, Toni?"

"The one about the poetry?"

"Correct."

"Do something more than special with your lives."

Irene nodded.

"Tomorrow is another day," he said."

"That was another film and another dialogue. *Gone with the Wind*, that was."

"And tomorrow we will be somewhere else," he said.

"And we need to decide where we are going, don't we?"

"Sounds good," Toni said.

He is nodding. I like that. But does his nod mean that he is ready now? Is he ready to change his life so that I can change mine?

"OK, dreamer," she said, "maybe it's time to wake up. Wakey, wakey, rise and shine."

"Which film is that from, Irene?"

"It doesn't come from a film."

"OK, dreamer…how did it go?"

"Maybe it is time to wake up," she said.

"From what?"

Irene could hardly hear him and, at the same time, she felt her body quivering, her face flushing and burning, and her mouth was dry and she was so confused she did not know where to begin even though there were things that she had been dreaming of telling him for so long.

"Nothing. My fault. Silly me."

"What is your fault, Irene?"

"Nothing, I think I might be getting a cold."

Toni stared at her.

"In the middle of summer?"

"Yes, a summer cold. People often ger summer colds. Ask Dr Fletcher."

"I don't see many people with colds."

"Then it's just me, Toni. I'm just not strong enough to carry on."

"Strong enough? To carry on with what, dearest?"

"Trying to be somebody else, trying to be a normal person in a normal relationship and coming here to live out a fiction, a fantasy, and a lie."

"So, what do you want instead, my love? What truth are you seeking?"

She believed she heard the sound of blood rushing through her body, and her body was now shaking and her skin was moist and she knew she was losing this first skirmish, this first Irene-outing of hers and she knew it would not be the last. There would be a next time and, maybe, a time after that until she could rest in peace.

"Nothing," she said. "It's nothing. It's all my fault."

"So, you want to be 'nothing,' my love, is that it?"

Irene did not know whether to laugh or cry and this internal conflict infused her voice with a shaky and squeaky quality that brought a heavy frown to Toni's face.

"I want to be myself, Toni. Miss Normal and she has a normal job in a normal supermarket and he …"

"What does he do, Irene?"

"I no longer know what he does – especially at night – when he prowls the streets and every sense is heightened and he listens for any sound of life and he hears it whether he wants to or not - anything at all, whether it be friendly or threatening."

"You make him sound like a cat, Irene."

"He makes up stories about himself. He watches films, acts them out and he becomes the hero. He lives in a never-never land of fantasy, half-truths and lies."

"Lies?"

"Exaggerations, perhaps. Yes, exaggerations."

"You are accusing me of lying, dearest."

"Forget it. Forget I spoke…"

Toni contorted his face, screwing up the courage to make a confession.

"Remember the story I told you a couple of years ago about my childhood – about my earliest memory?"

"One year ago, actually."

"Really? Just one year ago? Really?"

"You said something about sitting with your mother, listening to the radio and…"

"Switching everything off, right?"

"Right. What about it, Toni?"

"Well, it was a lie."

"Those slats, you said, they stirred a memory of Children's Hour, times at home with your mother in Goyt Bridge…?"

"Yes, those slats – the memory of my mother and of myself facing the dilemma – to remove the cigarette from between her fingers or leave it to burn her fingers. Well it was untrue – entirely invented."

"Why did you invent it, Toni?"

"Because it could have happened."

"But it didn't?"

"Probably not."

"So why did you tell it to me?"

She had no need to hear his reply. They had been here before, and the more he lied the easier it seemed to become.

"Just an interesting idea. It was fun and it could have happened, you see? But it didn't. It's just an idea, an interesting idea."

"What is an interesting idea?"

"Memory is an interesting idea, a re-enactment of things mostly forgotten," he said. "To think you remember feelings is a lie. You simply imagine what you must have felt in a situation you barely remember. You do the same. We all do the same. That makes me exactly the same as everybody else, doesn't it?"

The same as everybody else? Does that mean you think that everybody else is controlling and manipulative? Or do you believe that all the people around you are pathological liars.

"It is an interesting idea," Irene said.

"More tea of coffee," said the waiter.

"No, thanks," they said in unison.

She brightened and the sound of blood rushing through her body now faded and a plan took shape.

"I was talking to that interfering busybody Dr Fletcher yesterday. He says he thinks he knows who attacked Sonny Shaw."

"Thinks? Who does he think it was?"

"He didn't exactly say."

"What did he say – exactly?"

"He says he has been making enquiries about us."

"Enquiries? What sort of enquiries?"

"Enquiries," she said, "you know what enquiries are, don't you?"

"Depends on what type of enquiry you are making. Are you simply observing something or looking for patterns…?"

Irene waved an impatient hand.

"He says there is no record of us - anywhere."

"Really? Well, that's hardly a surprise, is it?"

"I suppose not. He clearly suspects something. He said he was there that night when Sonny was attacked."

"Really? And where did he say he was?"

"On a night walk. He said he was in the rose garden and found Sonny in a very bad state."

"Is that all? Did Sonny say anything to him?"

"Just one word."

"Really? What word was that – 'help'?"

"No, that was not the word."

"Was the word 'bastard'?"

"No, I'm afraid you are not even getting warmer."

"Then tell me what the word was, Irene."

"Pilot – he said the word 'pilot'. He said he thinks the word 'pilot' will help identify Sonny's attacker."

"Well, I wish him all the best and do tell him if you see him that we will, naturally, assist him if necessary."

"Of course."

Toni stroked his cheeks with his fingertips, rested his nose on his knuckles and gnawed – first on his thumb and then on his knuckles. Eventually, he swung his arm sideways and said:

"A pilot? So, the man is trying to limit our excitement, is he?"

"Stay calm, Toni."

Irene placed her hand over his to placate him but there was something warm, sticky and red on her palm and it had come from his hand to hers.

"Maybe, this evening, I will become Hannibal Lekter, but just for one evening."

"No, you will not. And you must leave him alone."

Tony was no longer listening.

"Did you know," he said, "that if you mix equal parts of petrol and frozen orange juice concentrate, you can make napalm?"

"No, I did not know that. Is that true?"

"That's right, one could make all kinds of explosives using simple household items.

"Really?"

"If one were so inclined."

"Which film is that from?"

"We just saw it. Maybe you have not had time to learn the lines?"

"*Fight Club*?"

He nodded.

"*Fight Club*."

"No, Toni, don't you dare. You have to stop now and I can help you."

"Guess there is no stopping me now, my love."

"But Toni…"

"Dearest?"

"Don't hurt anybody."

"Nobody will get hurt, my love, but my childhood taught me one important lesson."

"What lesson have you learned, Toni?"

She closed her eyes and hoped against hope that she was going to hear something different, something other, and something she could live with but as soon as she heard the abbreviated words, "don't," she knew what was coming and how it would finish.

"Don't just lie there and whimper when you get hit," he said.

"Get up, get on with it," she continued.

"Good girl," he said. "And how does it finish?"

Irene fought back her tears.

"And fight fire with fire," she said.

"Good girl."

"Toni, please don't do it, please…"

He put his hand on her arm.

"Don't worry, dearest. I am just going to singe the king's beard. Everything will be just fine."

8

Summer 1997 - Sunday morning

Dr Fletcher was settled, creased and pleated in his folding chair and he very occasionally let his eyes drift to the flashes on the horizon, the blanket of light, the wash over the sea, the distant rumblings and thumps of thunder and the clop of bat against ball.

"As you both surely know, Sonny suffered a traumatic head injury in 1993," Dr Fletcher said over his shoulder.

He can't look at us. Is he just focused on the cricket or have we done something wrong? Has Fletcher rumbled us?

Fletcher's striped-band-wheat-straw skimmer hat was balanced on his knee while his head analysed and collected data: the condition of the pitch, the fielding strategy and the run rate and, just occasionally, one arm rose in a gesture of despair at poor or unlucky play before jerking back into its usual place by his hat where his fingers clasped his knee.

"It goes without saying," he said, "that we all hope he will pull through, but there are causes for concern, as you probably know."

What on earth is the man doing here anyway?

"Here" was the Mini-Golf café, separated from Budleigh's cricket ground by a low picket fence, and both cafe drinkers and cricket enthusiasts were chatting, gesticulating, clapping and grunting, understated and under the cliff and not more than 200 metres from the seashore.

"Sonny faced a tenfold increase in the risk of stroke within three months of the initial incident," Fletcher said while watching a ball flying over the boundary. "He was lucky, but although he has survived, the risk of stroke will always be much higher for him than for those who have not suffered trauma of some kind."

He flicked his head towards Irene before turning it back to the game and its statistics and his gaze wandered over the cricket field to the distant pavilion, the white-shirt-and-trousered cricketers dotted around the pitch, the be-padded batsmen and the bowlers with their shoulder-rolling walk away from their crease.

And why is he telling us this? What has it got to do with us? Has he discovered our secret?

"I suppose you went to that school," Toni said with an upward thrust of his chin. "Learned how to play cricket at school, did we?"

Irene's attention drifted away from Dr Fletcher, passed over Toni and the confines of the Mini-Golf café until they settled on the road that led up the cliff towards the Victorian mansion that housed the boys of Budleigh Grammar School.

"At BGS? We did indeed learn the basics of cricket there," said the doctor with a vagueness that neither turned his head nor distracted him from what was happening on the field. Nor did he pay attention to the clink of teaspoon on saucer or to the low conversation drifting over the grass around him but he did participate in the occasional crackle of applause that followed the thwack that sent the ball rocketing over the boundary and into a distant rumble of thunder.

"And, later, we learned about cricket strategy," he said to the air. "Let me give you an example. You would not expect to see fireworks at this time of the morning, would you? There's ten minutes to lunch, and you don't want to lose a wicket now. After the interval the batsmen have to come out again and play themselves in once more. Less than two hours later and tea is coming. And so, that's a bad time to lose a wicket too, so better dig in again and don't lose your head even if those around..."

He broke off and signalled his approval at some event on the field by tapping the fingers of one hand against the palm of the other. Over his shoulder he said:

"And we learned sportsmanship, too."

His expressionless face, a celebration of a man's best behaviour, the uplifted chin at the cry for a decision.

"Just look at this."

Irene supposed that "this" meant the unmoving umpire, the batsman's stony-faced acceptance that his destiny was out of his hands, the stare towards the ground as if a solution to his impotence might be found between blades of grass; and the long walk back to the pavilion, acceptance of his fate and not even the suggestion of a complaint.

Irene looked up at the umbrella of seagulls squawking and soaring and diving and decided that the conversation needed shaking up.

"My father would have adored this," she said. "He loved to play cricket when he was a young man but like all those other poor boys, he was never the same after the war."

Fletcher looked her in the eye and requested information with a raise of an eyebrow.

Such a well-practised movement. What a vain man he

is.

"Others?" Fletcher asked. "You mean the members of the armed services?"

Irene nodded.

"He was posted to Palestine in 1946," she said. "A Grenadier Guardsman, he served in Haifa and Jerusalem until he was invalided home in 1947."

"A fine regiment," the doctor said. "But what happened to him? Why was he invalided home?"

"Ambushed by the Jewish underground fighters and…

"The *Irgun*?" "The Stern gang, daddy used to call them. The bastards shot him in the back."

"So sorry to hear this, Irene."

"He made a very good recovery, of course, and he had so loved his time in Palestine. Always wanted to go back and visit his friends."

"Bitter, was he?"

Irene nodded.

"And very angry," she said.

"Why did he never go back?"

Irene shifted her weight from one buttock to the other.

"He had health problems," she said with a biting movement of the mouth that suggested the words had been stuck between her teeth.

"Health problems, Irene? You can tell me, you know, after all, I am a doctor," and he smiled his "trust-me" smile, that smile which invited people to spill the beans, make a clean breast of things or get something off their chests.

"He was only partially mobile and simply stayed at home. Moving was too painful for him and he drank much more than he should have."

"Did he get violent, Irene?"

She wagged her head; tears filled her eyes and she nodded.

"Did you get help from your mum, Irene?"

Some things she told herself never to remember. Some things she refused to revisit, things like the smell of alcohol in the house, on the breath, in the sweat, under the armpit of a swinging hand or fist, and a whole generation of damage.

"My mum also drank," Irene said. "But I had my friend."

"And where was home for your mum and dad, you and your friend, Irene?"

And then it happened – it was out before she had time to realise it, but he had manipulated, blown the dam, forced the flow and weakened her resolve.

"Goyt Bridge," said Irene.

"Howzat!" shrieked the fielders as the befuddled batter turned to see the fallen bails and the crooked stumps and he set off on his crestfallen walk across the field to the clubhouse. Fletcher had gone for the jugular and she had fallen for it; he had weakened her resolve and taken a long shot and she had taken the bait, dropped her guard.

"Lancashire?" Fletcher asked.

Toni placed his hand on her arm and silenced her with a squeeze. He patted at his hair, crossed the ankle of one leg over the knee of the other leg and let his gaze drop between them to the floor.

"So, what's going to happen to Sonny Shaw," said Toni. "Will he die?"

Polite applause seemed to greet this question along with a freshening wind which air-cooled their cheeks and prompted a number of spectators to fold their chairs in preparation for rain. The doctor cleared his throat, prepared himself to change between a cosy chat about this and that with Irene and a factual exchange of 'yes' and 'no' and 'perhaps' with her husband.

"According to a new study," he said, "patients with injuries in which the skull bone was fractured, have a higher risk of stroke than those people who have never suffered head injury. The injuries Sonny received in 1993 were so severe that the risk of stroke will always be much - much higher for him."

A ripple of clapping, a rumble of thunder and chairs were unfolded again and the be-padded new batsman began his flapping walk to the face the bowlers. A muted conversation with the umpire, taking guard and a crease in the turf and the game was on again. A fine strike to boundary and a cap was lifted, applause was offered, faces were turned and politeness reigned.

"What would happen if Sonny were to die?" Irene asked.

"Well, let's look at a situation in which one person attacks another and beats him senseless. Hypothetically, you understand?"

"Of course," said Irene.

"Naturally," said Toni.

"OK – so it turns out that the victim is seriously injured but doesn't die. The attacker may be initially charged with aggravated assault or attempted murder…"

"Well played," shouted a spectator, and a bat is raised and claps are clapped and thunder clapped to celebrate the strike of a chap who had pummelled the ball to the boundary.

"Eighteen off one over," said Toni. "Good show."

"Did you play cricket at school?" Fletcher asked.

"Opening batsman," Toni said. "Scored the winning runs in the Northern Schools League back in 1969. Last over – last ball smashed over the boundary."

Toni winked at Irene and the doctor nodded and allowed his eyes to remain on Toni's face just long enough for him to reject a story that was as tall as his own forehead. And with the rejection, came raised brows and a crooked stare.

Why is he looking at Tony like that? He has rumbled him and he knows that Toni lives in a world of make-

believe?

Fletcher glanced at Irene, cleared his throat and continued with:

"However, if the victim later dies from his injuries, the prosecution may then charge the defendant with murder or manslaughter, depending on the circumstances."

Gosh, he has done his homework. What is he waiting for now? Applause?

"You know, not so long ago, the situation was very different. Shall I tell you about it?"

"Do, please," said Toni.

"Until 1996, there was something called the year-and-a-day-rule. This stated that an act of violence was presumed not to have caused death if more than a year and a day had elapsed between the violent act and the death."

"What does the law say now?"

"Now? If you are charged with the offence after a year and a day and it is shown that you directly caused the death of a person, then it is murder."

Another *howzat,* an expectant air, a raised finger and a ripple of applause sent a white-clad figure across the field. A player on the wrong end of super fielding, his fate had been sealed by a pluck from the air at short midwicket and now he was a batsman walking to the clubhouse and a nice cup of well-earned tea.

"But a murderer needs a motive and an opportunity."

"And you need witnesses," Fletcher said.

"Where on earth are we going to find those? Toni said, "It is a long time since the attack."

"Four years to be exact."

"Really?"

"Yes, really, and I can tell you something else."

"Do tell us."

"I hesitate to make accusations with no evidence

but…"

"No need to hesitate," Toni said, "just give it to us straight from the shoulder."

Dr Fletcher did hesitate. He inspected the faces of his interlocutors while Irene squirmed and Toni tensed and crossed his legs and re-crossed them and, for a short while, emotions were contained, body language screamed and silence transformed into anxiety, rejection and disunity, and deep inside Toni's cheek, a blood vessel pushed on the facial nerve near to the place where the nerve connected to the brain stem and signals were sent out to cause his cheek to twitch.

"You know," said Fletcher, "I think it is starting to rain."

His arms rose from his sides and he held out the palms of his hands.

"Yes," he said, "it is starting to rain. I must be quick. I can't put a name to an accusation until there is overwhelming evidence, but there are a few things you should know, for your own sake, you understand?"

"And what should we know…for our own sake?" Irene asked brushing a drop of rain from the end of her nose.

"It's time for tea," Toni said, with reference to the fine rhythm of village cricket. "Just in time I would say, before the rain has a chance to settle in. Two hours play, then a nice cuppa and a piece of cake."

"For our own sakes?" Irene said. "What do you mean?"

The doctor pouted his lips, inclined his head on one side and then the other before saying:

"Toni is right, my dear. When to strike out and when to bat clever? It is all about strategy. But let me answer you by saying that although I have no evidence just now, my stomach tells me that there is a connection between the attack on Sonny, the fire and the damage it did to my boat two years ago."

"It was a dry summer, 1995," Irene said. "Fire warnings were already in place."

Doctor Fletcher nodded.

"Indeed," he said. "Could be a coincidence, yes, that is true. But a doctor learns to look for the truth beyond the facts."

Toni shook his head.

"Then why…?"

"The facts are only half the story," Fletcher said. "To get the full story about an individual patient, a doctor has to see where and how a person lives his or her life. This information will often give the doctor the insights he needs to probe the essence of an individual's existence. In other words, a good doctor is well placed to look beyond the obvious to the real beginning of a story in order to draw the correct conclusions and suggest a course of treatment."

Toni uncrossed his legs, sat back on his chair, looked askance at the doctor and smiled a smile that was uneven, crooked and insolent, self-satisfied and scornful, something Irene might have described as a sneer except that a Tony-sneer was not a smile – it was a snarl.

"So, what happened to your boat?" Toni asked. "I'm not sure I know what happened."

"You don't know what happened? It was all over the local newspapers."

Of course, we know what happened but Toni is playing with us – play up, play up and play the game, Dr Fletcher

"Can't you just tell us?" Toni said.

"There was a major fire," the doctor said.

"My God, how awful," Toni said.

"Indeed."

"What is major?" Toni asked.

"It depends," the doctor said, "but in this case, the

word "major" can indeed be used to describe a fire which spread across two kilometres of fields and engulfed cars and a boat shed."

"How on earth did such a thing start?" Irene asked.

"We want it from the horse's mouth," Toni said.

Beads of sweat formed under the doctor's hairline while a salty breeze blew off the sea and tugged at his clothes. He shifted his gaze from him to her and from her to him.

"Apparently, the sun shone on a piece of glass and caused hay to ignite, but you know this, I…"

"Is that how it started?"

"Fire crews believe that the blaze started due to a pile of rubbish self-igniting. They think that a small tip at the bottom of a field contained glass and hay."

"And how," Toni said, "can that possibly start a fire?"

The doctor drew a deep breath.

"To be brutally honest," Fletcher said, "I don't think a piece of glass in a field of grass and hay had anything to do with this. In my opinion, it was started deliberately."

Irene and Toni tutted and shook their heads in unison. They exchanged glances and Toni said:

"I suppose you have evidence of this, Doctor Fletcher. We wouldn't like the wrong person to be arrested and accused now, would we? If there is one thing that makes my blood boil it is wrongful accusations and disproportionate punishment."

"Indeed, we would not like this to happen," Fletcher said, wiping a bead of sweat from his temple. "But people start fires for all kinds of reasons. They do it for the thrill. They do it to cover up evidence of a crime, to collect insurance money, for revenge and they do it because other people did it before them."

"So, you are saying it was arson?" Toni said.

"Arson? What sort of person would commit an act of arson?" Irene said.

Doctor Fletcher raised his arms in his Bill-and-Ben fashion and let them drop to his thighs and he said, while the fingers of one hand searched for the fingers of the other:

"What type of person? You really want an answer to this or are you simply making a comment, a judgement, a statement that does little more than express your own disbelief that people are capable of doing such things?"

"I'm just asking…"

"My research suggests," Fletcher continued with an impatient wave of his hand, "that an arsonist is usually a lone white male between 18-34 years old. He's disgusted or disgruntled with society, doesn't perform well at work, doesn't get along well with people, loves military and police paraphernalia, can't maintain a stable relationship, has some weird sexual problems and issues with alcohol."

"And do all arsonists fit this profile?" Toni said.

"No, but it can be useful to investigators in the early stages of their search for suspects. This was no small incident, you know?"

"Really?"

"Yes, really. The fire measured about two miles square and…"

"And involved fields and two sheds containing vehicles and one boat, apparently," Irene commented.

"My boat," said Fletcher.

"Sounds like pretty rotten luck," Toni said.

"As indeed is the weather," said Fletcher and he pushed himself to his feet, walked into the rain with hunched shoulders, paused and hurled parting words over his shoulder.

"Oh, I forgot to tell you what I think about Sonny's attacker. I think the attacker is known to us. It is just a matter of time and then…"

"And then?"

Fletcher smiled a weak smile.

"Have a good day," he said. "Enjoy yourselves while you still can."

9

Summer 2000 - Saturday evening

Irene stood at the closed door, pulled her shoulders back and her stomach in and listened to the remnants of human chatter and the pounding music which now reached out to her from the dance hall. A bitter-sweet mix of nostalgia and regret floated through and around her but the melodies reminded her, if she needed reminding, that tastes had changed since that first time 7 years ago, that the live band had gone with the plastic LP and the number of people doing Tango and Waltz had decreased when men decided to be spectators rather than participants and the turn of the millennium was the time to express yourself outside the formalised steps of classic dance. Freedom of movement was the watchword, freedom of thought the rallying cry and freedom of markets the slogan and gone was the backward-looking garb of 1993 and in came bright coloured clothing, skinny jeans, ear gauges, sunglasses, piercings, large belt buckles, wristbands, eyeliner, hair extensions, and straight, flat and dyed hair in colours like blond, pink, red, green, or bright blue.

Irene leaned forward, tottered on the tips of her toes, hovered for a second between outside and inside before falling back on to the heels of her trainers and frowning her attention at the not-quite-out-of-earshot chatter and the pounding melodies from the other side of the door.

The prima donna vocalist from the eighties and early nineties had moved aside to make way for the resident DJ and the people had responded and were younger and the music strange to her ears, but Irene could not help but wonder where it was all bound, how long it would be before a DJ walked into the next gig only to stand in silence while trying to convince the audience that his drunken shouts and gestures were real music performances to be appreciated. Irene could only say that, as a dancer, she was unlikely to be there. Dancing to the music of silence was not her thing, but nor was the effort by the artist she could now hear - a young singer telling her that he did not much care who she was or where she was from or what she did but adding the rider – as long as she loved him - but Irene sensed the dancers expressing themselves and self-conscious under sweeping lights and shuffling so close to her on the other side of the door that she felt obliged to join them in their Running Man, Macarena, Cha Cha Slide or Cabbage Patch.

If he is here tonight, which uniform will be wearing, which dance will he be dancing?

Another deep breath, blood rushing to fill her cheeks, shoulders back, head up; then, the music stopped, doubts appeared again and the usual dread stopped her in her tracks.

I am too old. When I fail at making myself look younger, I look pathetic. I am afraid. This is what I have convinced myself of – my own script, and I have been working on it since meeting Toni. I could have said 'no' and we didn't have to create him. Is this a script I was given at birth? Is he the Doctor Jekyll to my Mrs Hyde? Is he a monster of my making? I have doubts as myself, and I am fear in the shape of Irene Castle and neither can help me now.

She had dressed up in clothes which represented her version of vampire and which consisted of flowing black gown and a white streak running through her hair. Her face was caked in powder and her eyelids were shaded in purple. She rested her open hand on the door and her forehead on its knuckles.

The sound of the DJ at work reached out to her, his turntables turning, his microphone converting and working the crowd, saving lives from a broken heart and making the people feel alright, picking and mixing and selecting the tracks to please the visitors, turning it up with "Kung-Foo" and "Horny '98."

Irene shoved at the double doors and strode through them to the rhythm of some young rapper, and she realised she was hoping he would shut up soon.

Head up. Eyes front. You are 50 years old, so don't hide your bored facial expression and don't swing those hips because it looks ridiculous.

The rapper stopped dead in his tracks but Irene stifled a groan when he was followed by a woman singing about her sexual appetite.

"I'm horny, horny, horny, horny so horny…"

And her heartbeat remained stable when she entered this world which she would have preferred to avoid, but which she was now forced back into it because of him and his need to be forever young and forever with her. For 8 summers she had left herself at home in Goyt Bridge, and as Mrs Irene Castle she arrived in Budleigh Salterton to rekindle the fun, the lustful passion of her youth. But now, the years had caught up with both her and Toni and those years were to be confined to the scrapbook. Years of passion were already souvenirs, and the fabulous Mr Toni Burano and the wonderful Mrs Irene Castle were soon to pass away.

Keep smiling, Irene. Just go along with his wishes and think of the England you love.

She shook her head and her lips twitched their disappointment. The hotel ballroom was a-buzzing with swaying and leaping, bumping and jumping, a place where nothing compared 2 U and everybody was a *wannabe,* leaping around and doing that thing, that thing, that *thiiiing* they loved and people were rushing to the dance floor and turning out their best Running Man and Hammer Time as though they wanted to dance in one of those 90s music videos they should have danced in all those years ago - when they were young.

She placed herself in the darker shadow of a pillar and scanned the swaying and the swirling on the dance floor, looked for signs of him, his ease and grace, the thinning, grey-black hair and that battered dimple-when-he-smiled chin. A shifting shape, and Irene moved on with a glance of eye contact and a hand appeared, caught her inner arm with open palm and there was a tap on her wrist.

And to think, past experience had led her to expect blinking sequins and patent leather but here Tony was simply a part of the heaving crowd and there was no pause in the music because once the DJ had you, he was not going to let you go to the bar or the toilet, so one melody ran into another and Tony should have been there in front of her but it was not Tony who was tapping on her arm, not Toni who had cupped his mouth and was now shouting through the trembling air. It was Dr Fletcher and Irene had to shake her head, pull a face and wave her hand by the side of her neck to tell him that she could not hear him. She turned an ear in his direction, bared her neck and sidestepped towards him while he leaned forward and almost kissed her ear.

"I suppose you heard that Sonny died," he said.

Irene froze and mouthed a silent reply before finding her voice with:

"The beating?"

Doctor Fletcher raised his eyebrows and nodded and then she saw Toni – following the doctor as if he were the man's shadow – stuck like glue, riding piggyback and copying the doctor's movements, mimicking his questioning face and a movement of the thumb that indicated the bar area but she followed them both until they were out of the listening-and-dancing-only zone and the doctor pulled out a chair for her and took his own seat in a chair opposite.

"Yes, the beating," Fletcher said. "Medical experts have concluded that there was a direct link between his death last year and the attack made on him in 1993."

Irene touched at her ear and pulled at the lobe as if to clear it of a blockage. She said:

"Really?"

"Yes, really."

"And why," she asked with a shake of the head, "are you telling me this?"

"Because whoever beat him that night in 1993 is now a murderer."

Irene let out a long breath and fanned her face with her hand while Fletcher breathed in deeply and his breathing was a sick-sounding accompaniment to the pale skin, the swollen face, hanging eyelids, red eyes and droopy mouth.

"Cause of death? On the face of it – massive stroke, but, as you know, it is not as simple as that."

"No?"

"No."

What she knew, in fact, was that if she stood up to walk away, her legs might collapse beneath her and so she focused on the lyrics of the being-played song:

When I am about to go home, about to leave, don't you know I'll hold you close, can't you see?

"We all know that Sonny spent his life since 1993 in hospitals, rehabilitation units and at home and during the good times he was able to entertain and earn some money."

When I'm about to leave, I'll hold you close, can't you see?

"And here's the thing that has taken me so long. Thank goodness for modern technology. And do you know what I have discovered about you?"

Irene glanced at Toni. He had his elbow on the armrest of his chair, lounging sideways and he was scratching his cheek with the tips of his fingers while his chin rested in the palm of his hand and he seemed like a little boy wondering whether to eat this doughnut or that bun, or was he the little boy wondering whether he should remove the cigarette from between his mother's fingers or go outside and play, come back later and listen with mother? It was something of a surprise to Irene when Toni released his chin, sat upright and put the palms of his hands together and clasped his fingers as if this were a prelude to a prayer.

That our love will keep us close and you will always be with me, don't you see?

"Tell us, pray," Toni said, "what you have found out about us?"

The doctor lifted his arm and held the palm of his hand outwards as a signal that Toni should wait.

"The internet means that there is nowhere to hide, nowhere to go and no seaside resorts in which you can play charades, fool people and take them for idiots. You and your husband my dear have been outed."

Irene allowed the words of the song to pass them by before replying.

Don't you worry I won't let us break up and

disappear, don't you see a broken heart on a wall?

"By whom?"

"By whom?" Fletcher countered. "Don't you say "who by" where you come from and isn't it over yet, these games you both play?"

A song or a whisper on your lips before the dream, I promised you, don't you see, that I just wanna stay with you. Don't you see? Don't you see? Write your letters and dream your dream and I'll be home soon.

"You have lost me," Irene said.

"No, no. Can't you understand that I have found you?"

"I think you have lost the plot," Toni said.

"I have been researching into your lives and can you guess what I found? I am sure you can."

Irene shook her head.

"So, if you didn't know it already, widespread use of the internet has changed what I might call the mental substrata of Britain certainly and, maybe, of the entire world. A powerful new dream-world is being constructed before our very eyes and it is seductive and more unrealistic than anything the longer-established advertising and marketing businesses could come up with. On the other hand, our real lives seem to be becoming meaner and less prosperous. Consequently, the idea of the "perfect life" is born. Pictures of our friends enjoying endless parties and holidays and happy children are seeping into our envious consciousnesses. And the world is changing."

Toni's shadow appeared, leaning over them both, over the tablecloth.

"Get to the point," he said.

"The point is that I could find no mention of Irene Castle and Toni Burano or is that because you two have found the perfect way to ignore the internet and live a private life?"

When I am about to go home, about to leave, don't you know I'll hold you close? And I'll be home again one day.

"Perhaps you have found your own way of living a private life that harks back to a much simpler and online-less world but whatever you have found, you know as well as I that no guardsman by the name of Castle has ever lived in Goyt Bridge and nor have the man's relatives. You appear to be non-existent people with a non-existent past. Or are you entirely fake? Who exactly are you? What are you doing here and what was your problem with Sonny Shaw?

10

Summer 2000 - Saturday evening

The doctor shuffled towards the exit, and Toni scanned the table top, shifted his eyes from side to side and from top to bottom and did not glance at Fletcher's back, but all the while, his eyes reflected a film that was playing in his head and flickering things immoral or things that flew in the face of normality. But if Toni showed no apparent interest in Fletcher, Irene's eyes followed the man's back while he left the bar area and approached the exit door. The dome of his head was vast and looked to her as if it was the weight of ideas and thoughts which forced the neck to tremble and the legs to stagger.

When the doctor had disappeared and the exit doors were flapping themselves to a close, she put silent words to her thoughts.

He's sick, diseased, unwell…

Irene glanced at Tony as more ideas tumbled in her head and her inner speech spoke to her and shone a flashlight on her feelings and she found fear and uncertainty.

No, Toni, don't you go just yet because our time will soon disappear forever. I took you for granted without understanding you. You were always there for me as I was always there for you. Was "always" already determined when you were beaten for just being there by the people you should have been able to trust the most? Was Sonny beaten because he looked at the wrong person at the wrong moment and now is dead for his sins? Will you - please - stay with me for just one minute more and maybe we could stretch it to an hour or so, couldn't we?

"Leave the man alone, Toni. He is dying anyway, can't you see?"

Toni shook his head, narrowed his eyes and tightened his lips.

"God forbid," he said.

"Toni?"

"Have no fear, my dearest," he said, lowering his eyelids and wiping away her doubts with a wave of the hand. "The lines are already drawn and, rest assured, I have no intention of crossing them."

And let's make sure you do the right thing, Tony, because we should not go back in time and we can sit here forever and a couple of days because this is our last night and our last night is not the time to leave me alone so, don't go, stay with me now.

"One more year, my dear, and then it's over and we can move on."

She offered no argument to counter his proposal. He had already suggested, and she had agreed, that their love games had outlived their purpose and should come to a formal end the following year with a closing ceremony on the beach. The man who had given her sustenance of all sorts, the man who had protected her and the man whom she had protected his whole life long sat beside her now, and tomorrow he would meet and greet her for the last time and throw in the bedroom towel, put paid to the illicit hotel bills, bring an end to their love games, their little white lies and deceptions and Irene was already feeling the loss, recalling the fun they had enjoyed while breaking the norms of social conduct, in ripping apart the norms of relationships, but accepting that they could never have children – and there was no other place for their journey's end but the spot from where it had started twenty years previously.

"We'll meet on the bench, Toni," she said to him.

"Our bench then," Toni said.

"So long as it's there."

"It'll be there."

"So – let's sit here a moment longer," Irene said. "Perhaps, we could have one last lovers' dance?"

"What do you think?"

"You decide," she said, knowing that he disliked making decisions of any kind.

"I'll ask the DJ," he said.

One last dance, Toni, and then we can dispense with the past, with the games and with the illusions that worked and we can love, at last, in a natural union, with all our being and we can try with all our might till our days are done, but for now let's be here for a while.

His shadow was breaking over her.

"Would you honour me with a dance, Mrs Castle?"

"Delighted, Mr Burano," she said.

And so, the last dance was on, the final fling and the last waltz before the DJ packed up his equipment and went home. And then, footloose and fancy free, they would come back one more time and face the end of the road, the death rattle or the last hurrah. But Irene preferred the expression "swan song" to all the other expressions because she loved the idea of singing swans announcing their imminent departure and, although she knew it was just a myth, she loved to think that poetry proved more attractive than scientific method. The expression "swan song" described nothing tangible, and intangible was what she felt – how could you put a word to what she felt?

"Hold me tight, big man."

So, they danced, danced and danced with her arms around his shoulders and they danced and danced and his eyes were wild and happy and sparkling but she knew that the dance would become a past event, something to look back on and about which she could say:

"Ah, those were the days."

And this moment, like all moments, would either disappear into the great black hole of lost time or it would become long ago – long ago when they once danced and danced with eyes so bright and Irene knew that when, towards the end, the number of days shortened and she chased happiness down memory lane, it would be the idea of the long-ago him that she found – not Tony himself with his eyes so bright and his arm on her shoulder or was it her arm on his shoulder or was it someone else's shoulder entirely?

Will he say that I was a good companion. Is there a memory that he will always keep of me or will I forever be mixed up in his mind with saving him from the pain of his youth?

"I am just going out," he said. "I will be some time, but whatever you do, don't dance with anybody else and don't return a stare if you get one or there will be hell to pay."

And she watched him go, the subtle sway of the hips, the way he opened and closed the palms of his hands when he was nervous or angry. At the door, he turned and raised a warning finger before disappearing into the street.

11

Summer 2001 – on the seafront

Irene Castle stepped into the shade of the antique shop's entrance and she squinted down the street while allowing her gaze to travel to and through the rose garden and onwards towards the beach. She tried to detach herself from what she was looking at, remove her memories from the mix so that she could see everything as she had once seen it for the first time, but no matter where she stood, she was beset by flashbacks, prompts and reminders. She saw her meeting with Sonny on that sunny Sunday morning in the rose garden and heard Sonny playing his piano and delighting his audience and this flashback was but a tango-thrust away from Toni and those dance steps straddling midnight and, if she really squeezed her memory hard enough, she would see Doctor Fletcher way out in the bay and skimming over the water in his sailing boat and she was aware, acutely aware, of a feeling that she had never felt before the age of 40 and that feeling was connected to loss – the loss of love while it was mere butterflies in the stomach, loss of the opportunity to develop and grow, the loss of a future and the loss of another life and, more specifically, she saw now that she and Sonny were, perhaps, the love not lived, the road not taken, the kiss never taken, the pain never felt, a person never really known. The unlived love has no limits, never begins, has no time, never knows disillusion and never really ends. The beloved - usually distant, married, uninterested, or unapproachable - remains an object of indefinite idealization - a picture of Lilly, a longing with no hope, shivering in the dark - diamonds and rust.

And Irene was uncorked from her lovers' dream by the post-war ice-cream van shuddering past her with its pennants flying and a cloud of exhaust billowing. There were three lines of writing emblazoned on the side of the van: Roy Hart – Ices and Lollies - established 1925, and Irene wondered, as she often did, why "old" and "established" were associated with things that were good, reliable and trustworthy but when they were associated with people the words suggested boring, conservative and stuck in the mud.

Is the word "new" any better, Irene? Doesn't "new" suggest something untried and something to be wary of?

Whatever the answer, she knew that "new" was something she would need to get used to, because today was the first day of the end, the end of something, the end of something established, the end of something old, used up and irrelevant.

Irene looked, as she always did, always had done when she needed inspiration, towards the estuary. Budleigh Salterton was dissolving under the heat of the sun; the Victorian-green lamps that flanked the promenade appeared to buckle, and the distant pines, usually so proud and straight, now wobbled over the river bank. She squinted at the walls around her. Whiteness was broken only by the dark and worn tiles beneath her feet and, with the exception of the envelopes and junk mail splashed over the floor, the antique shop was bare. A shop that had once dealt in memories was now itself a memory and all she had said to him was:

"Meet you on the bench, Toni."

"Our bench then," Toni had replied.

The last bench on the promenade they meant, the one that overlooks, and will always overlook the river Otter while it washed, eddied and trickled over the rocks and into the sea. Irene looked at the house with the blue shutters, their slats cast sorrowfully downwards like his eyes and they reminded her of him and his story, his fiction, the fiction of his life but fiction was the life and soul of Irene Castle and Toni Burano, fiction was the life and soul of Budleigh Salterton and the heart of their existence, and make-believe was all around them and, without it, these sorrowful slats were dead things; they were shadows and Irene knew she could never, she would never, never, come back to the shadows.

The chiming of the church clock reminded her that time and tide wait for neither man nor woman and, taking a deep breath, Irene stepped into the sunlight and plunged towards the curtain of heat. At first, she was dazzled and screwed up her eyes so that they looked like purse strings. She discerned the outline of Roy Hart's van on the beach. In ice-cream yellow and blue, it was set at an angle, neither an acute one nor an obtuse one and not even a right one but an angle she described to herself as "crazy" because the van, like her current life, seemed about to topple over and reveal the unthinkable, the muck, the dirt, the damaged axles, the terminal rust.

She noticed groups of children, paddling and splashing, kneeling, scooping and building and she heard their screams and their laughter and this medley drifted over the dunes and across the water and reminded her of her time here 40 years previously. She had been looking for rocks to hold, rocks to give to her father to keep as a token of her love but she had given them to Toni to keep forever when he had come into her life as her special protector and he had stayed thereafter as her consort and he became her "special one."

And that is how you had wanted it, isn't it, when he became your special one, the one you needed for love, for understanding and protection from wicked and violent parents.

And Irene admired the sandcastles she saw now standing stout, thick of wall and defiant and mothers watched both castles and children from towels that claimed while the gulls squawked over them, and the sea lapped, swelled and waited. Then, as if from a dream, a voice said:

"Mrs Castle! Good morning to you. Nice to see you back again - and are you both dancing tonight?"

Irene turned.

"I'm afraid not," she said, but the person who had strode past, hand on hat and uttering the question was already swallowed in the curtain of heat.

Perhaps it had been the spirit of Sonny Shaw, who once loved to play the piano on the promenade and entertain the holidaymakers, but it could just as easily have been Dr Fletcher, who spent so many happy hours sailing his little boat in the pleasant bay

Irene knew that was not possible.

She wiped her brow and sighed in order to take the wind out of a developing sob. It was such a shame that Fletcher's sailing boat had foundered in rough seas the previous year, and the doctor had drowned. Senior coxswain of Budleigh Lifeboat and his crew did all they could to help. He said they launched in minutes and that they located the casualty but found him unconscious and not breathing. They tried life support on the lifeboat and returned to Budleigh to meet the land and air ambulance and coastguard. They worked on the man for around 45 minutes but to no avail and "sadly," he passed away.

"Everyone did a great job," the senior coxswain said. "Budleigh and the community came together and were very cooperative. The deceased was well known in the town and very much respected. We are unsure what caused the accident and, unfortunately, we were unable to stop his boat from sinking. It will probably never be known what caused the vessel to go down."

To her right Irene saw the gestures and she heard the excitement of children who were defending their sandcastles from the sea. Ahead, she thought she recognised the figure on the bench:

Or is it a mirage, Irene? Perhaps, he was always a mirage, a hopeless outlet for your need, your craving for love and affection.

At the end of the promenade, his pilot's blazer billowing outwards as it caught the breeze, her soon-to-be ex-lover was waiting.

Irene turned her head and Toni raised his arm and beckoned. As if the wind had abruptly changed direction, the clamour from the water's edge faded, and Irene felt cut off from a place far away. Taking his hand, they turned from the advancing sea and made towards the river. They watched the mullet nudging through the reeds, and they saw the swans gliding, and the leaves of the willow twinkled silver in the sunlight. They sat for the final time on their bench, and they felt the breeze caress their backs and blow onward over the water. The tide was up. The children were resting, thinking of the morrow, of bigger and stronger castles that would resist the waves. Children, breeze, river, and sea; unchanging and eternal, and Irene reflected that 10 years of role play had passed or were those years a dream?

Toni tugged at Irene's elbow and pointed to the restless water and the place where it merged with the sea and while they sat and gazed at the swirling current, they pulled closer and yet closer together; a dissolving vision in the sunlight. Silently they rose. Silently they moved off along the beach towards the curtain of heat. Slowly they became but spirits in the haze, and without a word, Irene Castle and Toni Burano faded away into a wonderland of memories.

12

Summer 2003 – Goyt Bridge

With regard to her life in Goyt Bridge, there are two things about which, and of which, Dot can be sure, and the first of these self-evident and certified truths has been known to her for more than 10 years and it is simply that customers see her as little more than a blob, a vague outline at the checkout, a shadow with neither shape nor form. The second truth, known to her as a certainty for an equal number of years, is that for those who queue with their fingers fumbling in purse or wallet, she is little more than the mechanical arm at the checkout, the slender but well-made arm covered in down and ending in a hand - smooth-skinned with sausage-shaped fingers that grip, lift and shove, pull and push packets of biscuits, bags of potatoes, the evening meal and the daily tipple. Cards are swiped, thanks are offered or heads are nodded, and she hears a voice with an away-with-the-fairies ear and she cocks her head and glances up as if someone else has uttered the words:

"That's fifty pounds and 33 pence, please."

Dot knows that this mechanical arm - or rather the brain to which the arm is attached by way of her shoulder and neck and head - registers that most of those who queue, purse in hand, will never see her as anything other than the check-out lady in the blue uniform who lives on the stool in front of the cash register and who never learned to say anything more than a few words - "hello" and "goodbye" being far and away the most common of these words - but the words "pounds" and "pence" and "thanks for shopping at Cutters," also making a confident and regular appearance. But she knows that these linguistic products are of little importance because Dot also knows that it would never occur to any of these shoppers to look any further than the end of the conveyor and take the chance, that she and Toni took all those years ago, and do something utterly different, turn their lives around and become somebody other, a somebody who was prepared to take an almighty risk and walk out of the supermarket and into another life of bliss, dancing, deception, sex and excitement. She often feels the need to stand up and assert herself, spill the beans, come clean and shout it to the rooftops but she knows that if she does, both the state and society at large would deem the relationship "unnatural" and come down on them like a ton of bricks.

But I want you to know that I am not just the moron at the checkout, don't you see? I took control of my life and I found happiness in him.

But while she grins at the next credit-card-in-waiting, she tries to ignore those frequent and nagging doubts that have the big tick-in-the-box of something confident and eternally true and as she gets older, these doubts and ticks appear daily in her eyes as the tiniest tears, and these tears get fuller by the hour and bear witness to the loss of things transitory like her lost father and her lost childhood innocence. Once upon a time, she had revelled in her father's power and her mother's glory and this power and this glory were beautiful while they stayed sober and peaceful, non-smacking, non-beating and caring parents but drugs and alcohol can make monsters out of the best of parents and what are a brother and sister to do when love deserts and violence comes knocking and thumping and bruising and cracking and survival becomes a day-to-day obligation and task for a couple of eight-year-olds called Dot and Bert?

But like any human being, Dot's longing and Bert's need to be seen, appreciated and loved never deserted them like their parents had clearly done, and hope and optimism took root one day while the two youngsters were playing in the garden, and Dot was convinced that in Bert a good father had risen from the dead and Bert believed he had discovered at last what he expected from a mother. That had been a time of innocence for them both, and innocence is a beautiful thing until suddenly, at some point after the first flush of adolescence, God and society forgot to bless this purity and this need for survival, and innocence became a forgotten milestone and a criminal act and the church clock strikes the hours.

"Clang," goes the church bell. "Clang," goes the bell of St Bedes. "Clang. Clang. Clang."

Between 1991 and 2001, and for ten whole summers, she left Dot Cutter at home in Goyt Bridge, and as Mrs Irene Castle she went to Budleigh Salterton to live a normal married life of fun, of dance and, she would add with a wry grin, a certain amount of lustful passion. But now, life, and indeed, an expectation of normality has caught up with both her and Bert and those ten summers are confined to the scrapbook. Years of passion are already souvenirs, and the smoke from their fire gradually melts into their twilight years. The affair is over, and the fabulous Mr Toni Burano and the wonderful Mrs Irene Castle, have passed away. But the wonder is, the thing that makes her mouth drop open in amazement is that they got away with it, got away with those ridiculous names, got away with murder.

When the church clock strikes five times, Dot Cutter is nodding off and sitting in her kitchen in Goyt Bridge while the lids on the cooking pots softly lift and fall and clatter in the billowing steam. Dot feels warm inside because her beloved brother will soon be back from his walk down by the canal, and he will probably be wanting his tea. And while she waits, dreams merge with daydreams and the house lies in silence until the moment his voice demands his tea, demands dinner, demands to be noticed, that she listens to his stories, his jokes, his threats, his ramblings so that Dot is sitting in a house and in a kitchen under clouds of steam and the weight of an expectant silence, a full silence, an on-the-edge silence that has already overstepped the mark because he is late and those demands for food and the sullen silences provoked by such a poor service are already present.

Better make yourself a nice cup of tea, Dot.

And Dot knows, as she shuffles towards the kettle, that she has to tell him today, that it can no longer wait and then she senses a presence behind her and the sense of menace is so overpowering that she is unable to move. She can only raise her eyes to the mirror above the cooker and she sees terror in her face and the reflection of her Bert standing in the corridor that separates the kitchen from the lounge and he is standing stock still but watching her every move through the gap between the kitchen door and its frame. She manages to convince herself that she does not hear him moving, does not see the kitchen knife and the way he is playing with it, like a baby with a rattle one moment, and the next moment, twisting the knife in a manner that suggests he would slash, slice, tear or rip up the air around him.

He watches her while, away with her protective fairies, she allows her thoughts to drift to a place of safety, of timber-framed houses, beautiful lawns and damsels in distress and she wonders - in her scatter-brained way - how many of her customers will ever have the wherewithal to step out into the sunlight as she and Bert did and take a trip to Devon. And for those who do, how many will have the stamina and the patience to reach the end of the promenade to see the benches lined up and facing the sea, and how many will actually use the unspoken offer or suggestion that a seat may be taken and the estuary admired. And of these, these that admire the estuary, she wonders, just how many will bother to read the most recent dedication plaques? Dot knows that only the curious will read the plaques on the seafront benches and let their minds wander, ask questions like: Who was that man? Who was that women? What happened to them? Will it happen to me?

And despite herself, despite her wildly beating heart, Dot glances into the mirror and she sees the rings under Toni's eyes, the tension around the nose, the twitching cheek and that paleness of purpose she notices whenever he is having one of his episodes.

"I just popped in to the iron monger, dearest."

"Yes, alright, dear. You put that knife down and I'll put the kettle on for a nice cuppa."

"They did a good job on the knife," he says.

"That's wonderful, dear. Now, I want to ask you something," she says.

"Yes, my love?"

"Do you want to go to Devon next summer?"

"Oh, yes please, let's go to Devon."

"You can see the place where Sonny played piano."

"Poor Sonny, but he was being beastly."

"And Dr Fletcher?"

"He knew too much, my love."

"Well then, we can look at the plaques on the benches."

"Which benches, my dearest?"

"The ones at the end of the promenade," she said. "Where the river runs into the sea."

And Bert looks up at the ceiling and searches his memory.

"Sonny Shaw who loved to play the piano?" he asks.

"Yes, that's correct, dear. And the others? Do you remember what's written on the others?"

Bert hums a melody and he puts a thinking finger on his forehead and he says:

"Dr Fletcher who loved to sail his boat in the pleasant bay?"

"Very good, dear. And the final one?"

And Bert scratches his head again until he raises his finger as if it were a magic wand and he wags it in the air.

"It says, 'In memory of Bert and Dot Cutter – alias Toni Burano and Irene Castle – brother and sister and two lovers of Budleigh Salterton,' doesn't it?"

"Indeed, it does, my dearest. Now do come here and I'll give you your tea."

Printed in Great Britain
by Amazon